I0666782

"Are you suggesting what I think you are?"

Shona was shocked at Marsh's idea.

"Making your fiancé jealous," he explained. "A collaboration between the two of us, a make-believe love affair."

Shona tried to imagine Calvin jealous. She *did* long to prove to him that *someone* found her attractive . . . and that someone would be Marsh Faraday. She answered, "You'll have to be a good actor," not mentioning that she wouldn't be acting at all.

"Then come here, woman." Impatiently Marsh pulled her toward him. "Let's start as we mean to go on." Shona did not resist as his mouth descended to hers.

"Marsh—" it was a token protestation "—there's no one to see now."

"Good." He was smiling faintly— was it with mockery? "We can practice our make-believe love in complete privacy."

LILIAN PEAKE
is also the author of these
Harlequin Romances

and these

Harlequin Presents

Many of these titles are available at your local bookseller.

For a free catalogue listing all available Harlequin Romances and Harlequin Presents, send your name and address to:

HARLEQUIN READER SERVICE,
M.P.O. Box 707, Niagara Falls, NY 14302
Canadian address: Stratford, Ontario N5A 6W2

Promise
at Midnight

by

LILIAN PEAKE

Harlequin Books

TORONTO • LONDON • LOS ANGELES • AMSTERDAM
SYDNEY • HAMBURG • PARIS • STOCKHOLM • ATHENS • TOKYO

Original hardcover edition published in 1980
by Mills & Boon Limited

ISBN 0-373-02404-5

Harlequin edition published May 1981

Copyright © 1980 by Lilian Peake.
Philippine copyright 1980. Australian copyright 1980.

All rights reserved. Except for use in any review, the reproduction or utilization
of this work in whole or in part in any form by any electronic, mechanical or
other means, now known or hereafter invented, including xerography,
photocopying and recording, or in any information storage or retrieval system,
is forbidden without the permission of the publisher, Harlequin Enterprises
Limited, 225 Duncan Mill Road, Don Mills, Ontario, Canada M3B 3K9. All the
characters in this book have no existence outside the imagination of the
author and have no relation whatsoever to anyone bearing the same name
or names. They are not even distantly inspired by any individual known or
unknown to the author, and all the incidents are pure invention.

The Harlequin trademark, consisting of the word HARLEQUIN and the
portrayal of a Harlequin, is registered in the United States Patent Office and in
the Canada Trade Marks Office.

Printed in U.S.A.

CHAPTER ONE

'OCEAN Rover Cruises? You'd like to speak to Mr Calvin Faber? Hold the line, please, and I'll call him.'

Shona placed the receiver on the telephone table and ran up the richly-carpeted stairs of the rented Georgian house they shared with three others in the heart of London. From behind each door came the sound of a musical instrument. Only to the outsider was the noise unbearable. To each musician who shared the house, contributing to the very high rent, the sounds were part of their everyday lives.

Calvin was, as Shona had expected, irritated at being interrupted while at practise. With the bad grace she had come to expect of him in the five or so years they had known each other—two of which she had been his fiancée —he removed the flute from his mouth and said, 'What now?'

'Ocean Rover Cruises on the phone.'

He frowned, looked thoughtfully at his flute, then placed it with gentleness on a table. 'Darn it,' he said, then more strongly, '*darn it!*' He was descending the stairs. 'They can't, not now, not while Jake's incapacitated.'

'Can't what?' Shona asked, following Calvin.

'Calvin Faber here,' her fiancé said into the telephone. He listened, said, 'Hell, I can't manage it that soon. Two weeks? But my accompanist is indisposed. What with? A broken foot, that's what. Of course I have to have an accompanist, you——'

'Sh-sh!' his fiancée cautioned.

'Unless,' said Calvin, turning slowly and staring at her, 'unless ...'

Shona frowned, growing apprehensive.

'Can you give me ten minutes?' Calvin asked. 'I'll call you back. Number?' He scribbled on a pad. 'Ten minutes.'

5

His hand lifted in a beckoning motion. 'Come upstairs, Shona. I want you.'

She backed away. There was no fear in her mind that he wanted her in the way most fiancés would want their wife-to-be. She might be wearing Calvin's ring, but he lived for his music. His hands and his mouth caressed his flute with far more expertise and excitement than they had ever done when touching her.

'I'm busy,' she said. 'I'm practising my——'

'Which is exactly why I want you. For practice.'

Shona followed, as she had almost from the moment she had met the young flute-player. Calvin Faber had, as people constantly told her, a great future. He opened the door to his room and entered. He sat her at the piano, placed a piece of music in front of her and said, 'Play.'

She did her best, but knew it was a mechanical effort. Calvin winced, then took up his flute, merging his playing and lifting the melodic harmonies he was creating until they floated over the piano notes, turning her tarnished-metal sounds to pure silver.

He lowered his flute and urged, 'More feeling, Shona, for heaven's sake!'

They began again and under the pressure of trying to please, she played a wrong note. He was on to her at once. 'I'm sorry,' she answered, and waited, hands together on lap.

He gave an exaggerated sigh. 'Try again.'

This time she earned his praise. She knew it was praise because he didn't curse her. 'That will do. It'll have to,' he said.

Shona swivelled on the piano stool. 'What will do? What's it all about? Will you please tell me? I have work to do for my class tomorrow——'

'No class tomorrow,' her fiancé said firmly. 'No classes, in fact, for the next three and a half weeks.'

Shona stared. 'You're joking!'

His mouth moved along the flute, going up the scale, 'No joke. A job. From the moment I ring that number back, we're engaged to play as the classical musicians aboard the luxury liner *Sea Wanderer*.'

'Ocean Rover Cruises?' Calvin nodded. 'Is that what the phone call was about?'

'It was about Calvin Faber and his accompanist, Jake Watson. But in view of the circumstances, it's going to be Calvin Faber and his accompanist, Shona Carroll.' He went down the stairs, saying, 'Either Ocean Rover Cruises like it, or they find someone else.'

Ocean Rover Cruises approved wholeheartedly. Which was how Shona found herself, two weeks later, aboard the great white ocean-going ship called *Sea Wanderer*, on a nine-day cruise to Las Palmas and Gibraltar.

'Excuse me,' said Shona to the masculine profile some distance above her head. Her arms, shoulders and hips eased and urged themselves into the gap she was making between people lining the rail of the ship.

The profile remained as serious and unmoved as if it were auditing the books of a multi-national company. It did not see the smile—bright, if slightly apologetic—which she had turned on it, and she gave up her attempt to charm it, turning instead to watch the waving groups of people who lined the Southampton quay.

A brass band was playing and, as the ship moved from its berth, the shining instruments glinted in the sun. The crush grew greater and she was pushed into embarrassingly close proximity to the thigh, hip and waist of the tall, indifferent man beside her. On her other side was a fair-haired, impeccably coiffured woman, almost as tall as the man. The feminine profile, however, seemed stirred by something from which the masculine profile probably never suffered—emotion.

'Moving, isn't it?' the woman remarked, smiling down at Shona.

The man, with whom she was now in almost disconcertingly intimate contact, turned his head at the woman's comment. He seemed to be about to answer her when he saw that she had spoken, not to him, but to the girl who was sandwiched between them.

'Very,' Shona answered, a little out of breath in her efforts to avoid being crushed into a cardboard cut-out of herself. Her eyes rose uncertainly to meet those of the man with whom her body was in danger of becoming lovingly entwined, through no fault of her own.

He, however, seemed to think it was her wish to wrap herself around him. Making no attempt to stop the ever closer pressure of her against him, the smile he shed upon her from his great height was not warm like the sun in the sky, but chill with a somewhat cynical amusement.

Receiving the full force of the gaze from his green-grey eyes, Shona would have reeled had the crowds now pressing from behind allowed her to do so. She said, tilting her head so that he could benefit from the full force of her cool stare, 'I'm sorry for wishing myself on you like this, but as you can see, it's being forced on me. Completely against my will,' she added freezingly.

'It's no good grumbling, darling,' said the fair-haired woman on her other side.

'Darling'? Good heavens, Shona thought, had she parted man and wife, man and mate, woman-friend and man-friend?

'Who's grumbling, Mother?' was the sardonic reply, as the full-lipped masculine mouth curved in a faintly derisive smile.

Mother? Shona could hardly believe her ears. This attractive blonde beside her, looking little more than in her late thirties, was this cold, icy-eyed man's mother? The green-grey eyes withdrew and, with hundreds of others, watched the waving people, the brass band, and the buildings growing progressively smaller as the tugs roped securely to the ship eased her gently into the Solent and then into the English Channel.

The passengers waving arms, growing tired, dropped to their sides. Their voices, hoarse with farewell cries, died away. The realisation was growing that they were on their way at last to a nine-day vacation to warmer places, leaving behind their homes, their jobs and the cares of their own particular worlds—and there was not a sad face among them.

'Is it your first cruise?' The woman's voice interrupted Shona's reverie. Her son remained where he was, but farther away, having been freed from contact from any other human being by the retreat of passengers to other areas of the ship.

Shona nodded, picking up a blue streamer, only to see it taken from her by the strong breeze. Another, scarlet this time, was pushed into her hand from the other side, and she gazed astonished at the aloof donor. 'Don't lose that one,' the man said easily, and turned his head as if he had already lost interest.

Her thanks were as faint as his smile, but she pushed the streamer into her handbag. Turning to the woman, Shona answered, 'I don't know what kind of a sailor I'll be, but I'm so excited I doubt if a storm force gale would upset me.'

The grey-green eyes came round with the turning head of the man beside her. His smile this time was touched with derision and a knowledge of all things sea-going which she, as a novice in the art of cruising, could not know. His superior air annoyed her and she gave her attention to the woman who really did seem to be his mother. The fact still had Shona mentally shaking her head.

'Travelling alone?' the woman asked.

Until now, Shona had informed people with a certain pride that she was Calvin's fiancée. 'No, with my——' Why was the word so difficult to get out? 'With my—companion,' she said at last, her right hand moving to cover the ring on her left hand. Her head turned defiantly to her left, her eyes lifting to meet those of the coolly amused man at her side.

And it's not that kind of relationship, she wanted to shout over the throbbing of the engines which were now working in earnest as the ship took to the sea completely under her own power. But the man merely smiled at her silent indignation. They watched the path of the ship as it moved determinedly on its way, as if it were as anxious as its passengers to shake, for a while, the shores of its mother-land from its hull.

'Have you cruised before?' Shona asked the woman politely.

'I've lost count,' was the answer. 'Eight, nine times—can you remember, Marsh?'

So the son's name was Marsh. Yes, Shona decided, look-ing covertly at him as he rested indolently against the ship's rail, it fitted, especially if the letter M was replaced by the letter H. There was about him, beneath that cool detachment, a hint of ruthlessness. It was there in his eyes, in the line of his mouth.

'I don't remember, Mother,' was the son's sighingly patient reply.

The woman laughed, taking her son's long-suffering at-titude in good part. 'No, I suppose you wouldn't remem-ber. After all, I am just one passenger among over fifteen hundred. In your position, what's one insignificant person, even if she is your parent?'

The words were spoken with amusement rather than rancour. 'You see,' the mother went on, 'my son's one of the——' The son's head turned quickly. Shona intercepted a warning look which passed from son to mother. Again the mother laughed. 'Now, you, Miss——' She paused. 'Did you tell us your name?'

'Shona Carroll.' The mother showed no reaction, but the son's head turned again, more slowly this time. 'I'm—I'm not just an ordinary passenger,' Shona enlarged.

'You aren't?' At the sardonic tone, Shona's head swung to her left, her dark brown hair lifting with the movement.

'I'm one of the performers—entertainers. I'm not sure of the proper description. My f——' Again her lips refused to form the word. 'My friend and I are under contract to Ocean Rover Cruises.' The woman's painted lips parted in silent surprise. The son made no visible response. 'He's a flautist,' Shona explained, 'he plays the flute. I'm acting as his accompanist. His usual partner's injured his foot, so he asked me to come in his place.'

'Well now,' said the woman, 'I wouldn't have guessed. A pianist! Would you, Marsh?'

'Never in a million years,' was the dry reply.

Shona retorted crushingly, 'What do you think I should do, Mr——?'

'Faraday,' the man she addressed supplied laconically.

'Mr Faraday,' Shona continued, spreading her hands across her chest, 'have "I play the piano" printed in capital letters across my tee-shirt?'

His mother laughed. 'Are you put in your place, Marsh?'

But Marsh Faraday's eyes had been caught by the diamonds decorating the ring on Shona's engagement finger. 'Is your fiancé travelling with you, Miss Carroll,' he asked, 'in addition to your—er—companion? Or was it friend?'

'Don't ask such personal questions, Marsh,' his mother chided. 'It's Miss Carroll's own private business how many men——'

'Private? When she's wearing that diamond-studded engagement ring? I was merely wondering,' with a cynical sideways glance at the girl at his side, 'if Miss Carroll has promised herself in marriage to three men at once—one man per diamond.'

'Take no notice of my son, Miss Carroll,' his mother commented good-humouredly, effectively preventing the sharp reply Shona's lips had threatened to fling at him. 'He's got as far as the engagement stage twice himself.'

'What happened?' Shona asked, tilting her face, with its piquant nose and wide, innocent-looking eyes, up to his. 'Did the ladies concerned take fright and back out? If they did, I must say I couldn't blame them.'

Had she got under this cool man's skin at last? His expressionless face gave little away, except for the faintest tightening of his lips.

Mrs Faraday seemed amused. 'I'll leave you two to carry on your squabble alone.' She looked around. 'I think I'll start unpacking before the dinner bell sounds.' To Shona she said, 'Are you first or second sitting?'

'First.'

'Like us. Isn't that nice, Marsh?'

Her son looked down, eyes narrowed, at the wind-blown hair of the girl beside him, at the slim-fitting dress, at the long-fingered hands resting on the deck rail, and said nothing.

His mother lifted a hand to Shona. Her son, accompanying her, left without a word.

'I've had a talk with the entertainments manager,' Calvin informed Shona as she approached her cabin. He was standing, flute in hand, in the doorway of his own cabin which was next to hers. 'Our first concert's tonight. Don't start getting hysterical,' as Shona's mouth opened in a soundless gasp, 'he said that if we hurry, there's a performing area on one of the upper decks—a fair-sized theatre but without tiered seating—where we can have about twenty minutes' practice. It's got a reasonable piano—not as good as the one you'll be using this evening—and there'll only be a handful of people about since most of them will be unpacking.'

Shona looked at her watch. 'And dressing for dinner. Calvin, we're at first sitting, and I must tidy up and change. There's barely half an hour left.'

The performing area of the place they called the 'theatre' was small. There was a narrow platform sufficient for groups to play, yet even those, Shona calculated, might well have to spill over into a larger raised space. Few plays, she imagined, were performed there, only set pieces with dancers and singers.

The piano was an upright model, too modern for her taste, but adequate for practice. She doubted if classical music had ever been played on it before. Her fingers ran over the keys, getting the feel and sound of it, while Calvin played a few scales on his flute.

'Right,' he said, after a few moments, and named a section of the first piece they would be performing that evening.

The ship rolled a little as Shona started to play, causing her to alter her rhythm. It had been beyond her control, but Calvin took his flute from his mouth and swore under his breath.

'You've got to get accustomed to the ship's movement,' he said bad-temperedly. 'Just for once you're performing as a professional.'

'I'm hardly an amateur, Calvin. All the qualifications you've got I've got, too.'

'It's experience, darling,' he answered unpleasantly, 'that little thing called experience that you lack. Not to mention —okay,' with a sigh, 'it doesn't matter.'

'Genius, weren't you going to say?' she said sarcastically.

He pretended to loosen his tie. 'I try to be modest. Now come on, for heaven's sake. Let's start again, and this time remember you're not on dry land any more. The ship's moving over a sea, not a stagnant lake.'

Stagnant, that's a good word, Shona thought, as she played the accompaniment mechanically, that's what's happened to my playing. Teaching kids music is all right for them, but does nothing for me. You're really a soloist, a voice in her brain reminded her, but you can't find a job because there are so few openings for soloists specialising in the piano. Unless—her fingers stumbled then righted themselves—you've got star quality, like Calvin, unless you become a concert pianist, commanding undreamed-of fees ...

The practice session was over just before the dinner bells sounded. With an irritable 'Come on, let's eat,' Calvin led the way from the platform, passing along one of the gangways to the door.

Seated in a dark corner in the back row was a tall man with black, wayward hair, firm pointed nose and etched lines betraying a worldly cynicism. Even without the faintly derisive look in his grey-green eyes, Shona would have recognised him instantly. All the same, she would have passed him by if he had not risen and made his way towards them.

Standing as he was, blocking their way to the swing doors, Shona had no option but to effect an introduction.

'Mr—er—Faraday, this is Calvin, Calvin Faber, my—my fiancé.'

Calvin nodded. Marsh Faraday gave a light bow. A mocking lift of the eyebrow preceded the question, 'And is he also the friend and the companion, or——' looking round, 'are they——?'

'No, they're not, Mr Faraday, and you know——'

'Hell, what's going on?' Calvin asked. 'Have you two met before?'

'On deck,' Shona said shortly.

'While Miss Carroll was taking a heartbreaking leave of her mother country,' Marsh Faraday commented caustically. 'And fighting off the streamers, of course, which Ocean Rover Cruises provide free of charge at each departure from Southampton.'

'O.R.C., Ocean Rover Cruises,' Calvin mused, running his fingers over his chin as if testing for tell-tale bristles. 'Part of the giant Ocean Rover Shipping Company. I looked the company up before we signed the contract. What did you say your name was?'

'Caught in the act, Mr Faber,' said the man called Marsh sarcastically. 'Marsh Faraday, one of the shipping company's directors.'

'You're not!' exclaimed Shona.

'I am,' was the reply, with a faint smile.

'Mixing business with pleasure?' Calvin queried.

'Or spying on the crew, from the Captain downwards?' Shona taunted.

'I guess I'd be wearing a false beard and dark glasses if I were doing that, Miss Carroll.' The keen eyes were harder now. 'I'm on vacation, if you must know. Accompanying my mother on hers, as you also know. Now, if you'll excuse me, I'll join her in the restaurant.' With a brief nod he left them.

'Yes,' said Calvin thoughtfully as they waited for the lift to take them to their cabins. 'Could be useful knowing one of the directors.'

'Look, Calvin,' Shona said irritably, 'I don't really know him. In fact, I don't care if I never see the man again.'

You're lying, said that persistent voice inside her, you're looking forward to seeing him again. Irritated with herself, she said angrily, 'Thanks to him, we'll have to go straight down to dinner. There won't even be time to comb my hair.'

Since it was still windblown from standing on deck, this annoyed her very much indeed. However, she consoled herself with the fact that no matter what she looked like, Calvin never noticed. When his flute was in his hand, he held it with loving care. When it was safely in its case, his thoughts were on the music he produced by the interplay of his mouth and fingers with its delicate and beautiful construction.

They were led to a table for four. When he saw the other two places set but not yet occupied, Calvin groaned. 'Good grief, they might have let us sit alone for meals! This cruise is a job to us, not a vacation. I hate having to make small talk when my mind's on my work.'

Their table was alongside a rail which looked down on the square sunken area of the restaurant. In the centre was a circular table seating eight people. On the brilliantly white tablecloth resting against a floral centrepiece was a white, narrow notice which read, 'Captain's Table'. Two of the Captain's guests were Marsh Faraday and his mother.

Shona drew Calvin's attention to the table placing of the man to whom they had so recently been talking, and Calvin tutted jealously. 'It's all right for some,' was his sour comment. 'Who's the slightly ageing but nonetheless ravishing blonde beside him?'

When Shona told him, his eyes could hardly have opened wider. 'His *mother*? I don't believe it,' he said at last. 'Who told you?'

'The woman herself. The son confirmed it. So it must be true.'

'She couldn't have been more than seventeen when she had him,' he remarked, studying the proud lift of the woman's head, the mature yet attractive figure, the pink, simply cut, yet flattering gown she wore. 'Like her son, a very superior being.'

'She really is a very nice person. I've spoken to her. Calvin,' Shona pushed her dark, still wind-blown hair from her face, 'is that how you like them?'

He frowned. 'Them?'

'Women. Is it blondes like Grecian goddesses who really get you going, and not brunettes with untidy hair like me?'

He picked up the menu as the waiter approached and Shona picked up hers. 'Don't be silly,' Calvin answered, and began selecting his dishes. Was it, Shona wondered, an escape from answering her question? Had she stumbled across the truth, which explained his lack of affection towards her? If so, why had he proposed to her? No gracious Grecian-type blondes among his female acquaintances. It was her subconscious mind giving her the answer.

No one came to join them at their table. 'Must have been a mistake,' Calvin mumbled, indicating the other two places.

'Or for the second sitting. Remember this is first sitting,' Shona pointed out.

As Calvin talked about the music they would be playing that evening, Shona listened carefully, but she could not prevent her eyes from wandering to the Captain's table. Towards the end of the meal, as her eyes lingered on the Captain's six guests—the seventh person at the table was his wife, it seemed—Marsh Faraday looked up.

His gaze went like the beam of a floodlight in the darkness straight to her face. He smiled, but his eyes stayed as cool as the evening air on deck. Shona reproached herself for allowing the touch of envy she felt to show in her expression. He had a perception too keen to have missed it. Hence the smile, no doubt, she thought sourly. Calvin was speaking so there was no chance to ask herself why she had taken such a dislike to Marsh Faraday after such a short acquaintance.

'We give our performance at nine-thirty,' Calvin informed her. 'It lasts for three-quarters of an hour.' He glanced at her dress, now bedraggled from the journey to the quayside from London, from her short stay on deck, followed by the rehearsal. 'You've brought one or two nice dresses, I hope?' he queried.

'What do you take me for?' she asked, irritatedly. 'I may not have played professionally as often as you, but I've had my moments as a soloist with different orchestras. Even if,' she finished a little tamely, 'they've been of the "Blank Town Symphony Orchestra" variety. Anyway,' defiantly as she intercepted Calvin's slightly patronising smile, 'some of the orchestras have been very good.'

'When augmented by local professionals, as some of them are.'

'All right,' she stood pushing back her chair, 'so I'm not as polished in my performances as you. But that doesn't put me on the level of a child having piano lessons against its will. At least I love the instrument I play!'

Shona had not realised how her voice had carried. A few people looked in her direction. As she swung round and made for the door she saw Marsh Faraday watching her and, as Calvin rose, putting his arm around her waist to placate her, watching him, too.

'Don't get so worked up,' Calvin urged. 'You'll exhaust yourself before we even start our performance.' They were going through the swing doors, now. 'You'll have me wishing more than ever that Jake Slater could have made it to the ship.'

Shona pulled away from Calvin's arm. 'So you've already wished it, have you? If you like,' she turned on him as they waited for the elevator, 'I'll disembark at our first port of call and you can ask among the passengers if any of them can play the piano.'

'Don't be a bigger fool than you need be,' was Calvin's ungracious answer.

As they stepped into the elevator, tears flooded Shona's eyes. This was her fiancé talking . . . She turned—to find herself face to face with Marsh Faraday. The elevator doors closed, His eyes met hers, but even as she dashed the tears away with the back of her hand, she knew he had seen them. She knew also that he must have heard a large part of the acrid conversation.

CHAPTER TWO

SHONA took some time dressing for the concert. In the next cabin she could hear Calvin practising on his flute. It would not take him long to prepare himself outwardly. His fair-to-brown hair would be combed flat in a few seconds. His square-shaped face would be freshly shaved, his hands scrubbed to whiteness, his nails excellently manicured.

His hands and his face, he always asserted, were the first and possibly the only things about him that people saw. He was of average height, his shape thickening just a little too much for his age, but since he watched his weight when he remembered, Shona knew he would never let himself become obese. It was the music he made, he would say, that had people riveted, and this, Shona had to acknowledge, was true.

Sometimes she wondered why she had agreed to marry him. He was there, she told herself, and that was probably all there was to it. She had great affection for him and admired him greatly as a musician. Affection, admiration . . . She never paused to think whether they were enough on which to build a marriage.

Alone in the world—her parents had parted as soon as she had come of age, and gone their own ways—she had reached out and grasped the hand that was offered her. For security, she supposed, for friendship, companionship and an end to loneliness.

Her own talents, she had known from the start, even at music school where she had first met Calvin, were not great. Average, Calvin had told her, maybe just a little better than average, but not good enough to carry her far in the world of music. Certainly not to the heights to which he aspired. And she had agreed with him uncomplainingly.

Her dress was long-sleeved, gathered at the wrists and

19

the waist. It was floral and filmy, the colours muted so as not to distract either from the music she played or, more important, his own performance, Calvin said. Her dark hair was simply styled, curling softly at cheekbone level and around her chin. Her make-up had been applied with a light hand, the perfume which she touched on at pulse points and behind her ears was reminiscent of summer gardens on warm evenings.

Knocking on Calvin's door and entering, she felt a touch of pride. This man was, after all, her fiancé, even though his demonstrations of emotional feeling towards her stopped short at a few kisses and a caress or two.

Even though he was only a little taller than she was, she knew that the women in the audience would look at him with something more than interest. She would be his shadow. It was, after all, sheer chance that she was on the cruise. Her one wish as they ascended in the lift from the deck where their cabins were situated was that Marsh Faraday would not be there to hear them play.

As they entered the Equator Room and walked along the gangway which had been formed by moving back the armchairs grouped around tables, Shona knew that her wish had not been granted. Seated at the side of a low table, drink in hand, was Marsh Faraday and his mother. There were others at the table too, but she was not in a state to notice them.

The ship was swaying and all she wanted at that moment was something to which to cling. She put her hand on Calvin's arm, but he shook it off. When they reached the grand piano, its lid propped open, she dropped the pile of music on to the piano stool. Resting her moist fingers on the shining wooden frame, she stood for a few moments, finding her balance.

A grey-haired lady at the front had turned her swivel armchair so as to gain a better view of the performers. The occasion was informal. The waiters still walked about taking orders for drinks and delivering them.

The lady, seeing Shona's face paling as she fought to

maintain her balance, asked if she felt poorly. Shona shook
her head vigorously, hoping Calvin had not heard. 'Just
haven't got used to the ship's movement,' she explained,
and the lady nodded understandingly.

Calvin watched moodily as Shona straightened, picked
up the music and moved away from the audience. He
walked across to her and said, keeping his voice low, 'What
are you worrying about? You'll be sitting down. I've got
to stand for the whole performance.'

His callous attitude stung. 'Don't worry, I won't let
you down. I'll play the best I've ever played.'

'You're not here to do that. You fade into the background, letting me take the stage.' The words were meta-
phorical since there was no stage. 'You play, like Jake, just
to give me backing. Surely you understand the basics of
accompaniment?'

'Give me credit for some intelligence,' she retorted under
her breath, striving to maintain the upward curve to her
lips as she sorted through the music. They were standing
at the rear of the piano behind an attractive arrangement of
flowers on a table nearby. It hid them from most of the onlookers. Except, as Shona discovered as her eyes roamed
anxiously over the people's faces, the vacationing director
of the Ocean Rover Shipping Company.

He was nearer than she had estimated and he watched
them, half hidden as they were, with hooded eyes. Low as
she and Calvin had pitched their voices, she was sure that
Marsh Faraday had caught the essence of their conversation.

A young woman whom Shona recognised as being a
member of the entertainments crew approached, smiling.
'When you're ready,' she said, 'I'll give the signal to the
waiters to stop serving, then announce you. Okay?'

'Introduce me,' said Calvin, appreciating her petite
figure and silky blonde hair—blonde again, Shona thought
—'we haven't met, have we?'

'You weren't around when your——' the girl looked at
Shona's ring, but must have decided that discretion was

more advisable than assumption as to their relationship, 'when I saw Miss Carroll looking lost and asked if I could help. I'm Toni Hardy. I'm under contract like you, I sing, dance, act, in fact do anything that comes my way.' Calvin's hand came out and held the girl's just a fraction longer than necessary. She smiled at him, eyebrows raised in query. 'You're Calvin Faber? Delighted to meet you. I've heard you play on the radio and so on.'

Calvin glowed. 'All flattery is welcome.'

Shona, placing the music in its correct order for playing on the rack above the keys, could not recall that Toni Hardy had commented on his performances, only mentioned them. When the girl asked, 'Ready now?' Calvin nodded and Shona led the way round the piano, to stand with Calvin facing the audience.

Toni Hardy had already indicated to the waiters that there must be no more movement from them. She spoke into a microphone, giving her message of welcome first to the performers and then to the passengers, hoping they would enjoy the concert of popular and light classical music that would follow.

Professionalism took over and, together with Calvin, Shona bowed deeply to the scattering of applause. She sat on the stool, arranging her long skirt with care. Calvin announced the name of the first piece of music. It was, he said, as were many of the pieces they would be playing, an adaptation for the flute and piano of a number of famous, and some less well known, musical works.

He then proceeded to electrify the audience with a performance of the Scherzo from Mendelssohn's *A Midsummer Night's Dream*. Shona kept her playing restrained, yet rose to every demand he made on her.

At the end Calvin bowed, extending his hand in the accepted fashion, towards his accompanist, at which Shona rose and bowed also.

Calvin played again and then once more before telling the audience that, while he took a rest, his accompanist would play for them. Shona played two short pieces, but even as she listened to herself playing, she knew the sounds her fingers were producing were mechanical and uninspired. It might have been the swaying of the ship, which seemed to have grown more pronounced, it might have been Calvin's performance which, that evening, had proved him to be on top form. It might even have been that she was tired after a long eventful day without rest.

Whatever it was, the applause at the end was polite, the faces who watched her bowing were smiling, mainly, she guessed, because her appearance and youth were pleasing to the eye. Automatically she looked in Marsh Faraday's direction. His mother was applauding, and smiling encouragingly. Her son leaned back in his chair, swivelling it slightly from side to side, a glass in his hand. As he sipped his drink, he gazed unsmilingly at Shona over the rim.

Shona sat again and Calvin, having announced the name of the next piece, put his flute to his lips. When the concert ended, Toni Hardy appeared from the shadows and made speeches of thanks to the performers and to the audience for listening. Shona gathered the music and the professional half-smile did not leave her mouth. Keeping up appearances, she thought. It's what I'm always doing. The strange idea had sneaked thief-like into her mind.

As the full lighting came on again, the diamond engagement ring glinted, catching her eye. Engaged to Calvin Faber who was edging towards fame and celebrity status, while she clung to his coat-tails, hoping maybe that some of his brilliance would shine on to her ... Momentarily she covered her eyes. Her mind was playing tricks, revealing unsought-for truths while under the influence of fatigue and a rolling ship on roughening seas.

Calvin was talking to Toni Hardy. She heard the words 'schedules', 'programmes', 'the required number of performances'. Tucking the music under her arm, she walked as gracefully as the ship would allow along the gangway towards the swing doors. The noise level had risen, waiters were darting to and fro like bees seeking nectar.

'Miss Carroll!' The voice was feminine and familiar.

'Join us for a drink. I'm sure you must need one.' It was Mrs Faraday, patting the empty place on the couch which was next to her son's chair.

Assailed by an unexpected weariness, Shona smiled and complied. To reach the seat, Shona had to get past Mrs Faraday's son. He was a formidable barrier. Shona found herself easing her legs between the low, hard table and the son's equally hard knees. As the table was fixed to the floor and therefore could not be pushed aside, it was impossible to avoid physical contact with the man.

He, however, seemed as obstinately immovable as the table, which meant that Shona's legs had of necessity to press against his in order to reach her destination. The taunting smile on his face added to her embarrassment. Her brown eyes were flashing anger signals at him, when the ship took it upon itself to roll badly. Caught completely off guard, Shona found herself lunging towards Marsh Faraday, finishing up sprawled face down, in a very undignified fashion, across him.

His willing arms closed round her and since her head was somewhere in the area of his ribs, the material of his jacket effectively muffled the laughter and exclamations of sympathy which came from people all around her. The experience of being in such intimate contact with the man with whom, since she had met him, she had done nothing but argue, was so pleasant, yet so disturbing, that she found herself struggling indignantly, then struggling reluctantly, to break free.

For his part he was doing his best to keep her there. By the time the ship had rolled to the other side, righting itself at last, she had managed to extricate her body from his embrace. As she stood unsteadily, with the music still miraculously clasped under her left arm, she heard her name uttered in an irritable voice.

Lifting a shaking hand to tidy her hair, she turned to find Calvin looking at her unbelievingly. She knew what he was thinking. 'If I can cope with the ship's movement, why can't she? It's something a performer has to learn to cope with.'

'Sorry,' she mumbled to her fiancé, 'it was the——'

'The truth is, Mr Faber,' her long-legged, exasperatingly relaxed tormentor said, 'your fiancée seems to have taken such a liking to me that she couldn't control her mating instincts and just threw herself on top of me.'

As the laughter rose again from the surrounding group, Shona turned on him. 'It's not true and you know it,' she protested. Seeing the broad grin on Marsh Faraday's face, she realised how foolish she had been to rise to his taunt. 'I'm ready to go when you are,' she told Calvin, and was about to negotiate her way around the offending table without again making contact with Marsh Faraday's knees, when Calvin announced,

'I'm taking Toni for a drink. Okay?' Without waiting for an answer, he rejoined the fair-haired girl and they disappeared.

'Now you'll have to stay with us,' Marsh Faraday's mother decided. 'No woman in her right mind buys herself a drink, certainly not when there are able-bodied males with large bank accounts around!'

Marsh Faraday watched as Shona seated herself beside him. The plump, balding man on her other side said, with a wink at Shona, 'You'll have your son annoyed, Verity, if you discuss his private business in public.'

The man about whom he was talking responded blandly, 'As long as it's my private business she discusses and not my private life.' His lazy look strayed to Shona, his eyes, tracing the arched line of her brows, her inviting mouth, her rounded chin, then lowering to dwell on the floating, essentially feminine material of her dress.

Her head lifted, meeting his eyes boldly. If he thinks, she told herself, he can reduce me to simpering adulation of his male physique and magnetic good looks by assessing me as if I were being auditioned for his harem, then he's mistaken.

Marsh lifted a hand to a passing waiter. 'A drink, Miss Carroll? Dry Martini?' He ordered, having gone round the group.

'I enjoyed the concert, Miss Carroll,' Verity Faraday said.

'Me, too,' echoed a white-haired woman who appeared to be the plump man's wife. 'I thought you played very prettily, Miss Carroll.'

Shona smiled weakly, closing her eyes for a few seconds. 'Prettily', when she could, had she let herself go, played with such fervour that her performance would have prompted far more complimentary words than the woman's faint praise. As Calvin's accompanist she had restrained herself, always she was restraining herself, having to stay both mentally and physically one step behind her fiancé ...

Her eyes fluttered open to find Marsh Faraday's gaze resting thoughtfully upon her. From her fingers curling around the music, along her arms to her shoulders the tension crept, finally holding in bondage the whole of her body. Even a look from him disturbed her, while the memory of those few moments when so much of her was in such close contact with so much of him made a faint shudder course through her nervous system.

The waiter returned and distributed the drinks.

'That young man,' the white-haired woman passenger was saying, 'what was his name? Calvin something. He played extremely well.'

'He'll go far,' her husband agreed.

'Yes,' said Shona, faintly smiling and taking a drink from her glass, 'I think he plays brilliantly.'

As she lifted her drink again and felt it swirl down her throat, the ship lurched again and the brown liquid that was left in her glass splashed on to her dress.

'Oh, dear!' Mrs Faraday exclaimed, producing a paper tissue from her bag and handing it to Shona. 'That lovely dress. Will it stain the material?'

'I—I don't think ... I mean, I hope not.' Shona was rubbing at the strong-smelling damp patch.

'The cabin steward,' said the older woman, 'he'll attend to it. Won't he, Mr Faraday?' The woman had addressed him as if he were the ultimate authority on all matters connected with the organisation and running of every ship owned by the Ocean Rover Shipping Company.

'If he doesn't,' was Marsh Faraday's sarcastic reply, 'I'll do it myself.'

Shona's head came up, her flashing brown eyes clashing with his. It was the mocking look that greeted her which brought together in a great, engulfing whirlpool the events of the past three weeks, from receiving the shipping company's invitation which had been followed by days of constant practice, then leaving home that day, joining the ship and eventually giving a tension-racked performance.

Calvin had disappeared. The ship's movement was proving alien to her system. It had vindictively swilled alcohol on to one of her concert dresses. And the man whom, curiously, her mind was blaming for it all was sitting there relaxed, smiling and altogether being thoroughly obnoxious . . .

Shona rose, still clasping the music. 'Please excuse me.' Again she had to manoeuvre herself between the table and his legs. This time she stared fiercely down at him, but the trembling of her mouth she was unable to control. As he saw her emotional state, the cynical smile was replaced by tightened lips. He moved, allowing her easier access to the gangway.

She called 'goodnight and thank you for the drink' and hurried to the swing doors, this time reaching them. As she pushed her way through, the ship lurched again and she staggered to a halt, bracing herself for the moment when the floor would give her back her normal balance.

A hand rested on her arm. She turned her head slowly, expecting to see Calvin. When she saw Marsh Faraday, she said emotionlessly, 'I'm all right, thank you,' and started walking towards the stairs and down to the deck where her cabin was situated.

The hand moved to her shoulders and guided her to the lift. It came almost at once. The doors opened and Marsh led her in. He seemed to know the deck she wanted because he pressed the correct button. As they descended, he did not move his arm. In a strange surge of feeling, Shona felt a longing to stand closer to the man.

Before her body could let her down and move of its own accord, the doors reopened and her companion eased her out. He showed every sign of taking her to her cabin, and she said hurriedly, 'There's no need.'

The ship, however, rolled again. Shona found herself staggering across the corridor, pressing the music to her chest with one hand and reaching out to the handrail with the other.

'It's plain there's every need,' Marsh Faraday's deep, firm voice observed.

He appeared to know exactly where her cabin was. She fumbled for the key and he took it, opening the door. 'I can manage, thank you,' she said, but he took the music from her, put it on a table and looked around the cabin. He seemed satisfied that the cabin steward had performed his duties correctly, having been in during dinner to change the daytime couch into the bed in which she would sleep that night.

'Is your fiancé's cabin next door?' he asked. Shona nodded. 'Then if you need help he'll be near enough to give you any assistance.'

Closing her eyes, she tried to envisage Calvin caring enough about her to drag himself out of bed to come to her aid. But she could not conjure up even one picture of Calvin playing nursemaid to his fiancée.

If I married him, she thought, I'd certainly be marrying him for better, for worse, since I know his failings almost better than I know his assets even before becoming man and wife ... *If I married him!* Surely that should have been 'when'? There had been no doubts in her mind—until now.

To cover the silence during which her thoughts had chased each other like raindrops down a window, she said, 'That's what the cabin steward is for, isn't it?'

'Cabin stewards must rest some time, but there's a night watchman who would do his best to help. I'll have a word with him.'

It was a reminder of the man's status and this produced

inside her a giant wave of resentment. 'Please don't bother, Mr Faraday,' she said, 'I'm just a passenger among hundreds. I don't want special treatment.'

'Maybe I should remind you,' as he spoke his eyes held no warmth, 'that you're on this ship as part of the entertainments team, under contract to the shipping company to perform at an agreed number of concerts for the duration of the cruise?'

'Please forgive me,' Shona said sarcastically, walking to the stool which was pushed under the cosmetics compartment of the dressing-table, 'for forgetting my place as a temporary member of the *Sea Wanderer*'s crew.'

As she pulled out the stool, the ship rolled. The floor's refusal to stay level unbalanced her again and she found her hands on the seat with her arms stiffly supporting her sagging body.

'Thank you, Mr Faraday, for coming with me,' she said. 'I'll be all right now.'

At that moment her energies seemed to desert her. She walked unsteadily to the bed, collapsing on to it and curling up uncaring that the man was still in the doorway. Without even the strength to tell him to go, she closed her eyes and let herself drift. It was some hours later that she stirred, finding the bedcovers over her. Only the light above the bed was still on.

Her face felt flushed and she pushed aside the bedclothes, wondering who had taken the trouble to pull them up. Had the same person removed her shoes? Hurriedly she looked down and discovered with relief that in every other respect she was dressed as she had been all evening. Nothing else had been removed.

Had Calvin come in and, contrary to her expectations, acted the nursemaid? Knowing Calvin, Shona thought it was very unlikely. Yet surely Marsh Faraday would not have bothered to make her comfortable? She recalled his reminder of the reason for her presence on the ship and accepted that he might have taken the trouble after all. Not for her sake, but to make sure that she, together with Calvin, adhered to the contract and that she in particular kept her side of the bargain.

Daylight brought no change in the weather. Shona slid out of bed, finding her slippers with her feet. I feel better, she thought, I've adapted to the rolling and rocking of the floor. And then she stood up. Something happened in her head and her hands went up to it as if to hold it in place.

Carefully she walked to the window, pulled aside the curtains—and saw the wild, billowing sea. Quickly she turned away. Taking her robe from the door, she pulled it on. 'Whatever happens,' she told herself, 'I must keep going. I'm not an ordinary passenger, I'm being paid for the work the shipping company expects from me.'

There was a tap at the door and the cabin steward turned the key, bringing in her early morning pot of tea and biscuits.

'Beautiful day,' he said cheerfully, putting the tray on to a pull-out table. 'How are you today?'

'Wishing I could copy you and carry a loaded tray across a cabin without spilling a drop of anything.'

He laughed. 'Practice, that's what it is,' he said, whisking from the room.

Shona poured the tea and drank, watching the too-full cup deposit some of its contents into the saucer. She finished the tea but pushed the biscuits aside. Then she stood, bracing herself to cross the cabin. As she opened the bathroom door, it swung from her hand and hit the chest of drawers behind it. It then swayed back and hit her shoulder as she stepped into the bathroom.

Having washed and dressed in white shirt-blouse and slacks, Shona sat on the stool and determinedly opened the lid of the cosmetics compartment. She would put on make-up and behave as if there was nothing wrong, no see-sawing floor beneath her feet, no swinging wardrobe doors, no splash of the sea's spray against the window.

The mirror before her showed a pale face which made her all the more determined to bring some colour into it, even though that colour might be artificial. Despite the fact that her hand shook as she applied mascara and eye-shadow, adding a bright lipstick as a finishing touch, the result of her efforts was not unpleasing and she closed the lid with a satisfied snap.

There was a tap on the door and Calvin let himself in. 'You've got too much lipstick on,' was his first comment.

Shona smiled invitingly. 'That's to make you want to kiss it off.'

'I don't like it.'

She thought of the blonde girl called Toni Hardy. 'Is there anything about me you do like?' Shona flared. He shrugged, keeping his eyes on the wet tray and unused biscuit packet. 'Did you enjoy your evening with Toni?'

Again he shrugged, then counter-attacked. 'I understand you found someone to escort you back to your cabin.' There was a faint sneer in his voice.

'If you're referring to Mr Faraday, it was very kind of him to bring me. I was feeling faint.'

'I should think you were, after chucking yourself all over him in the Equator Room! A man with his money and position is enough to go to any girl's head.'

The ship rolled particularly badly and Shona staggered, finding herself grabbing the bedclothes. Calvin had let his body go slack, taking the movement easily.

'You'll have to learn to deal with the ship's rolling and pitching before this evening. We've got to perform again.'

'I can only do my best, Calvin.' His careless attitude incensed her, but before she could snap back an answer he said, his eyes everywhere but on her, 'I've been thinking—it might be better if it's not generally known among the passengers about our engagement. It's more—well, professional if we're regarded as completely separate performers. Even married couples use different names, so——'

'Don't strain your intellect thinking up more excuses,' said Shona, her voice shaking, not with tears but chagrin. 'You would have much preferred it if I hadn't had to come with you, wouldn't you? Then you could have gone as far as you liked with that Toni girl.'

'Jealous?'

Shona considered the question and answered quietly, 'No, I'm not.' And, curiously, she realised she meant it.

'Why can't you be honest and say "yes"?' Calvin challenged, red-faced with annoyance and pained vanity. He turned to go, missing the look in Shona's hurt yet angry eyes.

'Okay, Calvin,' she said as he reached the door, 'from now until we get back home, we're free of all ties.' Pulling the ring from her finger, she flung it to the back of a drawer.

CHAPTER THREE

As the breakfast bells sounded, Shona knocked on Calvin's cabin door. There was no reply. It seemed as if Calvin had gone to breakfast alone. A tight knot of tension formed inside her as she walked along the corridor. Grasping the handrail and bracing herself against the constant swaying, she reasoned that it was not unhappiness at Calvin's careless attitude which was tying her emotions into knots, but irritation that he seemed already to be dissociating himself publicly from her.

Whether it was the result of a subconscious effort to boost her confidence or whether it was spontaneous and genuine, she did not bother to discover, but a sudden sense of freedom infused her body. A defiant spurt of pleasure rushed through her, and it took no more than a few moments to discover the reason.

If only for the duration of the cruise, she had symbolically ended her engagement to Calvin. Contemplating her ringless hand, she thought, I'm free again, if only for nine days or so, to look at other men. Were there, she reflected, any 'other men' she wanted to 'look at'? At once she knew the answer, but she would not even whisper it to herself.

She threaded her way through the groups of tables and saw that Calvin was already seated there, consulting the menu. Two other people were doing so, too, the missing passengers from last night's dinner. When she saw who those passengers were, she almost turned and made for her cabin again.

Since the ship's dipping and rising action had increased rather than lessened, she had no choice but to continue. Reaching her chair at last, she saw that Mrs Faraday was sitting next to her, while her son sat opposite. Calvin was on her other side.

Marsh Faraday's dark hair looked as if it had been blown about by a walk on a windy deck. The grey-green eyes which looked at her from over the top of the large menu card were topped by thick brows, one in its normal place, one arched, as if the smile on the lips was mocking.

'I hope you slept well,' the hidden lips said.

It's a chance, Shona thought, glancing at Calvin's indifferent expression, to have my revenge for my so-called fiancé's interest in another girl. Not to mention an opportunity, she realised with some satisfaction, to play Marsh Faraday at his own game.

'Very well, thanks,' she answered, gazing as he was over the top of her own menu card, 'and thank you for covering me up. Oh, and for removing my shoes.'

Calvin's head jerked up and he stared from one to the other. A mischievous smile flitted across Mrs Faraday's attractive features.

'It was no bother,' Marsh commented, lowering his menu. 'Any time you need assistance getting into bed, just ask ...' With a touch of malice, he watched a slow flush creep over Shona's face.

The ship had started to roll again. Its movement was even more noticeable now than when she had washed and dressed. No matter how she tried to tell herself otherwise, there was no reasoning away the effect it was having on her. Her head felt badly balanced on her shoulders. It was almost as if it didn't belong to her. Lowering the menu card to the table, Shona raised her two hands to cover her ears as if the action would restore the world to normal.

Marsh had noticed and his taunting attitude left him. His mother followed his gaze, becoming immediately sympathetic. Calvin, too, looked at her, but sharply, without commiseration.

'What's the matter?' he asked.

'It's something to do with the organs of balance,' Verity Faraday contributed. 'Poor you, Miss Carroll.'

'Call me Shona, and I'm sorry, but—Calvin, I'm not pretending.'

'Go on deck and get some fresh air,' her fiancé advised dismissively, returning to studying the menu. 'You've got to get used to it. We're not ordinary passengers, as I keep telling you.'

Marsh looked with something like contempt at Calvin's indifference. 'The shipping company is not inhuman, Mr Faber. If one of our entertainments staff is ill——'

'She's not ill. It's all imagination.'

'Wrong,' returned Marsh. 'Only in a small percentage of passengers affected like this is the trouble due to psychological reasons.'

'The chief officer told me,' Mrs Faraday remarked, 'that it's a force eight gale. Go to the ship's surgeon, dear. He'll give you something to help you. It's wonderful these days how they deal with this sort of thing.'

'Have something to eat now you're here,' Calvin muttered, with a trace more consideration. 'It might just help.' To Marsh, 'Have I said the right thing this time, Mr Faraday?'

He had spoken caustically and Marsh's eyes hardened, but he did not answer. The waiter brought toast and stood waiting, pad in hand, for the order.

'You're looking a little better, dear,' Mrs Faraday commented. 'So how about fruit juice? Orange?'

Shona nodded. The waiter asked if there was anything else, but she shook her head. He went round the table, writing down the dishes.

'Hi.' A slim, fair girl stood beside Calvin. 'The amount you drank last night, it's a wonder you haven't got a hangover up to here.' With the back of her hand she touched her chin.

Calvin looked at little uncomfortably at Shona, then laughed. It's the first time, Shona thought, I've ever seen Calvin embarrassed. By the time Calvin had thought of an answer, Toni Hardy had gone, leaving behind the scent of her perfume.

To fill in the glancing silence and the awkward, unasked questions, Calvin said, 'Seems a force eight doesn't affect *her*.'

Marsh answered, moving his cutlery around, 'She's travelled as a crew member on a number of our cruises. She found her sea-legs long ago.'

Calvin looked meaningfully at Shona who said, as sourly as she felt, 'Lucky Toni Hardy.' Verity Faraday offered Shona the plate of toast. Shona was about to shake her head when Mrs Faraday pressed, 'Just one piece, without butter. You really should eat something, you know.'

Reluctantly, Shona accepted a triangle of toast, but even the crackle of its crispness set her teeth on edge. As she drank the orange juice, watching the others happily consuming their eggs and bacon, the ship pitched and rolled badly.

She pushed back her chair, putting a hand to her white face. 'I'm sorry, but I must go—get back to my cabin. Don't let me stop you . . .'

Waiters stood impatiently aside as she rushed headlong for the swing doors. Someone came to walk beside her and miraculously the waiters drew away with a smile to leave a clear path. An arm came round her shoulders.

'Calvin,' Shona murmured, 'go back to your breakfast. Just leave me alone.' Then she looked up—and up. Calvin never was as tall as this man. And no wonder she had suddenly been treated so deferentially by the waiters!

'Please go back, Mr Faraday,' she mumbled. 'I never meant to trouble you, nor anyone. I can find my own way to my——' As she waited for the lift, the ship swayed and Shona swayed with it, her body falling against that of the man beside her.

Opening her mouth to apologise, she closed it again. He was holding her where she had fallen and the hardness of his hip and the toughness of his thigh penetrated to her deepest senses, in spite of the way she felt. His arm was tight about her and for a fleeting moment she allowed herself the luxury of relaxing against the strong dependability of him.

As she looked up, so he glanced down at her. He gazed into her pale face, no smile lighting his eyes. His lips were a taut line, his jaw squared with something like anger. The lift arrived and with one or two passengers, they stepped in. The presence of those other people prevented conversation which, Shona decided miserably, was fortunate. She was in no fit state to take on the chin a lecture as to how wrong it had been for her to join the ship as a performer if she was such a poor sailor.

In her cabin she sank on to the bed which, like magic, had become a day-couch. The cabin steward had carried out his duties with speed and efficiency. Marsh Faraday stood, hands in the pockets of his casual slacks, looking reflectively down on her bent head. At last he said, 'Shall I call your fiancé? It's his place to be here, not mine.'

For a few seconds her eyes flared. 'I didn't ask you to come. I wish you would go. *I wish you would——*' A hand went to her head. 'I'm—please excuse me.' The bathroom door rammed shut behind her.

When she emerged, her hands held her face and she was vaguely aware that Marsh Faraday had remained. She collapsed on to the couch, drawing up her legs and lying lifelessly on her side.

He stretched across her to take the telephone receiver from its hook. 'Steward?' he said. 'Faraday speaking. Ask the doctor to come to Cabin 15, "Y" deck, will you? Yes, tell him I'm requesting the visit. For Miss Carroll, one of the entertainments crew. Thanks.'

'I could have gone to him,' Shona said through her fingers which were spread over her face. 'Everyone else will have had to go to his surgery. Why not me?'

'You,' said Marsh Faraday with false patience, 'are not "everyone".'

'Don't tell me—I'm special,' she muttered with an attempt at sarcasm. 'I've got to be up and about by this evening. There's a concert, which means I've got to carry out my part of the contract.'

'Will you kindly shut up? Reserve your energies, both

mental and physical, for recovering from your malady. Don't waste them by trying to exchange smart quips with me.'

There was a brisk knock and the doctor entered, followed by a nurse. After a few quiet words with Marsh Faraday, the doctor, a kindly, middle-aged man, asked Shona a few relevant questions. He explained that the nurse would be giving her an injection which would make her sleep for three or so hours, and this was to be followed with the taking at intervals of tablets which the nurse would give her.

As he left he said comfortingly to Shona, 'You'll find all this a great help. We'll soon have you back to normal. Just relax and sleep the injection off.'

Shona nodded, already sleepy, and thanked him as he left with the nurse. Marsh did not go as Shona had expected, and said, hoping he would take the hint and leave, 'Thanks for what you've done, Mr Faraday.'

'The name's Marsh.' He went to the door.

So he was going now? Shona thought. Instead of the satisfaction she expected to feel, there was a dip of disappointment as deep as a wave trough. The door opened and he called, 'Steward!'

As if the man had been hovering in case of need, the steward appeared.

'Have you a spare quilt? Miss Carroll must be covered over.'

'Not on this deck, sir. There may be one not being used in a suite.'

Marsh said impatiently, 'Bring one from mine, Cabin 61, "W" deck. There's an extra bed in it. My steward will let you in.'

'Certainly, sir.' The steward went away.

'Have you got a suite, Mr Faraday?' Shona mumbled, the injection beginning to take over.

'The Seascape Suite. Does it annoy you that I should travel in luxury?' The question was asked with a smile.

Shona could hear it in his voice even though her eyes were closed.

'It goes against the grain.' She was not completely in control now of the words her lips were speaking. Her eyes fluttered open to see him looking down at her, arms folded, legs flexible so as to yield to, not resist, the floor's constant movement. He was plainly completely at home on board. 'But a man in your position in life—not to mention the shipping company—well, it would be expected, wouldn't it, that you'd be given the best?' A smile flitting across his lips was her only answer. 'I suppose,' she went on, her words slurring a little now, 'you own a luxury yacht and all the trappings of a rich man?'

'Why shouldn't I? What I do with the money left to me by the tax man is surely my business?' His words sounded indulgent, not sharp as she would have expected in normal circumstances. No doubt he was humouring her, waiting impatiently for the steward to return so that his responsibility would end.

Drowsily she thought, Responsibility? But he had none towards her. It was Calvin who ... Of course, the contract to play, her official involvement with the shipping company—Marsh Faraday was making sure that the company did their duty by her, not only so that she would keep the passengers entertained, but ...

'Are you afraid,' she roused herself to say, 'I might claim damages?'

He frowned. 'Explain.'

'For—well, lack of proper medical attention from Ocean Rover Cruises, the other party to the contract.'

'The medical attention you're receiving,' he said sharply, 'should be covered by your own and your fiancé's arrangements for medical insurance before you embarked.'

Shona sighed, unable any longer to carry on a rational conversation. The steward returned, and Marsh took the quilt from him. 'Leave this to me.'

'It's my work, sir. I'll——'

The sentence was cut off, probably by a dismissing move-

ment of the shipping company director's head. The door
closed. As hands held her ankles, even from the depths of
her enforced tranquillity, she shivered. Sandals were removed and the quilt came down, covering her body.

'You seem,' she mumbled, 'always to be taking off my
shoes and tucking me in.' Her hand lifted, in an effort to
reinforce her thanks. It was her left hand. Its descent to the
bed was impeded by fingers which closed round her wrist.
The touch of Marsh Faraday's hand was becoming disturb-
ingly familiar.

'No ring?' his receding voice asked.

Shona was too far gone into sleep to answer.

Dragged from the depths of sleep, Shona surfaced be-
wilderedly. It took a few moments for her to decide where
she was and how she came to be there. Somehow the bed
was moving, a cupboard door banging, the picture on the
wall thumping now and then against the wall.

Something had awoken her—a hand on her arm, shaking it, a voice, loud, then louder, saying her name. 'Are you
feeling better now?' It was not a sympathetic query. 'It's
lunchtime. Are you coming with me?'

'Calvin,' Shona replied, words tumbling over themselves to be spoken, but staying right where they were, in
her mind. 'Not hungry, no lunch. Couldn't eat.'

'You've got to start eating some time today. There's a
performance to do tonight.'

'Miss Carroll won't be working this evening, Mr Faber.'
The voice, coming from the doorway, was quiet yet held
unmistakable authority.

Calvin swung round. 'Hell, so what am I supposed to do?
Play the flute *and* the piano?'

'Mr Faraday,' Shona's distressed eyes sought his, 'I can't
let Calvin down. I'm here as his accompanist, so——'

'Then let him find a replacement. The doctor has advised no normal food today. Dry toast, dry biscuits, tea.
Nothing more. Later, if you feel like it, you can get up, but
certainly no performance. You understand, Mr Faber?'

'I suppose my preferences don't merit consideration?' Calvin asked sulkily. 'That fact that I want to perform——'

'Haven't you any consideration for your fiancée's state of health?'

Calvin turned a dull red at Marsh's cutting tone and with a 'See you later' to Shona left the cabin.

Shona held out her left hand. 'Hadn't you noticed?'

'I had,' Marsh answered, 'but when I asked about it, you went to sleep on me.'

A smile gave a touch of life to her pale face. 'Sorry about that.' A small silence, then she explained, 'Calvin thought it would be more—professional if we didn't display our relationship to the public. He said that even married couples use different names.' Even to her, it sounded a feeble reason.

'You're not yet married, which means your names naturally remain different. So why the suspension of the engagement?'

Shona inspected the white mark where the ring had been. 'Dare I mention,' she said with a frown, 'the name Toni Hardy?'

'I told you, that girl gets around. Surely Faber isn't taking her seriously?'

'He likes blondes. When one comes in sight, his eyes latch on to her. Blondes act like a magnet to him.'

'And you,' his voice had softened a little, 'are dark, dark brown.'

Brown eyes lifted to his, serious, large and, at that moment, inward-looking. 'Precisely,' she replied.

There was a tap on the door and the newcomer entered. 'Marsh, so this is where you are.' Verity Faraday stood beside her son. 'How do you feel, dear?'

'Better, thank you,' Shona answered.

'All the same,' Marsh instructed, 'no getting up, no food and no performance this evening.'

Verity lifted her blonde head and looked proudly, yet amused, at her son.

'How Marsh loves throwing his weight about! Even as a

small boy, he gave his mother and father orders.' Marsh smiled, folding his arms and waiting with a sigh for the maternal talk to end. 'When his father died, Marsh came into his own, taking over as man of the house, putting me in my place.'

Marsh gave her a reproving look, but she continued to smile lovingly at him, catching at his arm. There was no doubting the affection which existed between mother and son.

'How old were you, Mr Faraday,' Shona asked, 'when your father died?'

'Twelve, and for pity's sake, make it Marsh. I've put you to bed twice. Don't you think we know enough about one another by now to be on first name terms?'

Shona blushed and Marsh's mother laughed at her blushing, which only confused her more. 'You have to keep my son in his place, Shona,' she commented. 'Women?' She tugged at his arm. 'He can't keep his hands off them.'

Marsh said exasperatedly, 'I never thought I'd hear my own mother utter such outrageous falsehoods about her only son.'

As Verity patted her son's arm and said, 'Have it your way, dear,' Shona yawned. Verity was immediately contrite. 'There's plenty more sleep inside that girl, Marsh. The gale's still having fun with the ship,' as she spoke she was forced to cling to her son for support, 'so the best thing is for her to do as the doctor ordered and stay right there.'

Shona turned appealing eyes to Marsh. 'Do I have to?'

Marsh's gaze lingered on her sleep-flushed cheeks and disordered hair. 'My mother's right. Another hour or two——'

'Half an hour,' Shona compromised, and with a smile, settled down again. Verity waited at the door. 'Marsh?' Shona said his name shyly. 'Tell Calvin I'm sorry, will you, please?' His jaw moved as if with displeasure. 'After all,' she went on, 'I am still his fiancée even if I've temporarily stopped wearing his ring.'

'Don't you ever stop crawling to him?' Marsh said with

contempt. 'How long do you propose to allow him to use you as a mat to walk on? All your married life? Haven't you any fight in you?'

No one had ever spoken to her in such terms and she raised herself on to her elbow. 'Fight? Mat? Crawl? What are you talking about? If a woman's engaged to a man who's been described even by the severest music critic as a "near-genius", isn't it right that she should let him take precedence over her? Put up with his moods? Try to adapt herself, her work, her technique so as to enhance his?'

'My God,' he joined his puzzled mother at the door, 'they say that love is blind, but where your feelings for your fiancée are concerned, that's only the half of it. You're deaf, dumb *and* dim-witted as well.'

'And you,' Shona flung after him, 'are a stupid, unfeeling brute!'

The door closed with a bang and Shona sank back to the pillow fighting the tears which had sprung from her depths to her throat and finally to her eyes. Why they were there she was too distressed and too weary with approaching sleep to work out.

A persistent knocking on the cabin door had her pulling herself out of her heavy sleep. Once again it was Calvin who wakened her.

The 'fight' which Marsh had so contemptuously accused her of lacking began to stretch and waken in her brain. It had always been there, but circumstances and her vocation had lulled it to sleep. In the world of music, emotion was reserved for the performance of that music. Self took second place, even in the virtuoso and the musical genius, and there were precious few of those.

'What do you want this time?' she began, when she saw the smile on Calvin's face and the tray in his hand.

'How do you like your new cabin steward?' Calvin asked, placing on a table the tray containing the prescribed dry toast and tea.

His behaviour was so out of character that Shona wondered, for a moment, if he had been drinking. Remembering then that Calvin rarely touched alcohol, she sought for another cause. It came to her at once, but she played along with him, preferring to converse with a smiling, pleasant Calvin than a moody, uncharitable one.

She struggled into a sitting position, putting the back of her hand to a warm face and pushing back straying hair. 'You're not wearing uniform,' she humoured him. 'That won't do.'

He laughed—really laughed—and Shona found herself reacting as if she had had a shock. 'You're to stay in bed for the rest of the day,' he told her. 'Doctor's orders.'

Hoping she sounded playful, Shona answered, 'Don't sound so pleased, Calvin. It means I won't be able to play for you this evening.'

'That's okay. I've found a substitute.'

'Oh? Who would that be?' She took a piece of toast from the plate he offered her and bit into it, making a face at the bland, uninteresting taste. However, it went down better this time and, indicating that she wanted another piece, realised she was feeling much stronger.

'Toni Hardy.'

The toast stopped just short of her mouth, which came open with astonishment. '*What?* I thought she was a compère?'

He walked about the cabin, his attitude that of a man who had just won a fortune. 'Toni's very versatile. She sings, dances, plays the piano. Not serious stuff, usually, but we had a practice this afternoon. If I play some of the simpler, light classical pieces, she'll manage. Anyway,' his faint sneer annoyed Shona, 'with such an undiscerning audience as we shall get, they won't recognise a wrong note or two.'

Shona shrugged, staring unseeingly at the quilt which still covered her. If a girl as musically uneducated as Toni Hardy obviously was would suffice, then what was she, Shona Carroll, trained and qualified pianist, soloist whom nobody—or very few—wanted, doing on the cruise at all?

Calvin left at last, having supplied her with two cups

of weak tea. He even bent down and kissed her—admittedly
it was chastely, on her cheek—but the action surprised her.
She was startled by the ringing of a telephone. Tracing it
to the telephone receiver which hung vertically on the panel
beside the bed, Shona lifted it and said a hesitant, 'Hallo?'

'I'm speaking from the steward's office. Have you eaten?'
Shona's pulse rate, which had been slowed considerably by
the tranquillisers which the doctor had administered, began
to labour upwards towards normality and beyond. 'Yes,
thank you.'

'Did you appreciate your new cabin steward?' The sarcasm was faint but perceptible.

'My fiancé, I suppose you mean. Yes, thank you.' She
would give Marsh Faraday no encouragement. It would
take her some time to forgive him for his merciless criticism
of the way she conducted her personal relationship with
Calvin.

'Your instructions are,' the arrogant voice went on, 'to
make yourself ready for bed.'

'I'm feeling better, Mr Faraday. I don't feel like getting
into bed.'

'Look, I said make it Marsh.'

'I don't feel like "Marsh-ing" you either, Mr Faraday.'

Smiling, she hung up the receiver and swung her legs off
the bed. Carefully she moved herself into a standing position. The ship still rolled, but either she was growing accustomed to it or the force of the gale had lessened. But there
was no doubt about how she felt—weakened, empty but
determined to get out of the cabin at least for an hour or so.

The door came open and Marsh regarded her. 'Preparing
for bed?' he asked curtly.

'You're not my keeper, Mr Faraday. I can do as I choose.'

'Your keeper I may not be, *Miss Carroll*, but you're
travelling as an employee of the shipping line and as such,
you will obey the orders of a representative of that shipping line. Get it?'

She clasped her hands in front of her, little-girl-like, and
said, 'Yes, Mr Faraday.'

Something in her half-smile and falsely servile manner must have angered him. 'Stop goading me, Shona!'

At the sound of her name on his lips, her heart jumped, but she would not be pushed around any more, no matter who did the 'pushing'. Looking at him through fluttering lashes she answered, 'I'm making myself into a mat, Mr Faraday. I'm crawling, Mr Faraday. After all, you are an influential man, aren't you? A director of Ocean Rover Shipping Company, and heaven knows what else.'

The ship swayed and Shona, to her dismay, swayed with it. With her legs still weakened and slowed down as she was by tablets and injection, her reactions were not fast enough to hold her upright. If Marsh had not moved like lightning, catching her, she would have hit the floor.

She was in his arms, close to him again as she had been when, the evening before, she had been thrown by the ship on top of him as he sat in a chair. This time there was no feeling of urgency to pull away. This time there were no onlookers—only her subconscious mind, which did not seem at all disturbed by its owner's proximity to the very male physique of the man who had caught her.

'Th-thanks,' she stammered, making a token attempt to pull herself from him. The ship swayed again and his arms tightened, pulling her closer. She clung to his shoulders and closed her eyes. The rolling movement, and in addition, feeling her breasts crushed against his chest, her hips against the ridged hardness of his, her thighs caressed by the sinewy toughness of his, was intoxicating.

It was almost as though they were dancing together, yet they stood like carved stone figures, inseparable by events or time. The sea, having had its fun, settled down for a while. Marsh's braced legs relaxed, becoming even more disturbing as they moved against hers.

Shona's eyes came open, the tip of her tongue tried in vain to dampen her dry, cracked lips. There was a thirst inside her which the two cups of tea Calvin had given her had not assuaged. As she looked up into eyes which were crinkled a little yet touched with mockery, she became aware of the source of that thirst, aware too, alarmingly, of the way, the only way, that thirst could be satisfied.

The full lips on which her eyes were lingering started to speak. 'Do you still feel disinclined to "Marsh" me, Miss Caroll?' He spoke softly, his eyes busy examining her bright eyes, her arched brows, the white teeth which her slightly parted lips revealed.

'I——' Her fingers played with the open neck of his blue shirt. There were dark hairs beneath which she longed to touch, but her other self told her that they were strictly out of bounds. She glanced up, smiling provocatively into inscrutable eyes. 'I still need reassuring that it's right and proper for me to——'

His mouth hit hers with a force which ground her lips against her teeth. All of her yearned to respond, but her other self said, 'No. Remember Calvin ...' As the kiss went on it became increasingly difficult to remember Calvin, or anything else. Calvin had never kissed her in this way, nor had any other man.

Yet that irritating other self won the battle. With a giant effort, her self-control came into operation. Her body grew stiff in his arms. Feeling her resistance, Marsh slowly lifted his head, leaving his arms around her. As her muscles had tensed, so his hold had tightened. Now, in his anger at her body's repulsion of him, his arms became like cruel bonds.

'After that supreme bit of "I'm yours for the taking" act, you have the cheek to imply, with all the female "no-go" signs you can muster, that you want me to get the hell out of here?'

His hands had moved to her arms. In his anger his nails were making piercing dents in her flesh. She wanted to cry out but stifled her responses. In a strained voice she said, 'My ring may be in the drawer, but I'm still an engaged woman.'

'The devil you are!' He threw her from him and she staggered, only just managing to right herself. 'Not judging by the way you pressed yourself against me when I caught you, the way you kissed me back when I kissed you. You felt like a woman who'd been wandering in the desert for months, devoid of all male contact—and do I mean contact!'

'That's not true,' she flung back, knowing he was right but knowing, too, that nothing would make her admit it. 'It—it was reflex action, pure and simple. I—I hated it, really. I hate the—the very taste of your lips.' With the back of her hand she wiped her mouth.

The ship pitched again and again she was thrown off balance. This time he let her fall. She went backwards across the bed, hitting her head against the telephone and radio panel as she went down. A cry escaped her and she lay there, pale from the impact, weak from lack of food, still not free of the heaviness which the doctor's remedies had induced.

In spite of her pallor and her lassitude, Marsh did not touch her. After looking down at her contemptuously as she lay limply with her eyes closed, he left her.

It was some time later that Shona awoke, to discover from her watch that she had slept for over three hours. It was after nine-thirty, too late for going anywhere.

Yet she couldn't stay there alone, hearing outside the laughter, the brisk sound of feet, the shrill voices of children going to bed. The cabin had become too confining, everyone who had called on her too much like prison officials, forcing her to stay there. A hand went to her forehead, then explored the area which had come into hard contact with the wall panel. There was a painful bump, nothing more.

Her mood bordering on the defiant, she washed and found a floral dress with a frill bordering the low, rounded neckline. A layer of make-up hid her paleness, a white, lacy shawl added a touch of flattery. Pulling on evening sandals, she tested the floor. It was steadier now. As long as her legs were strong enough to take her to the lift, she could reach whichever deck she wanted. If only she did not feel so empty . . .

It was almost ten o'clock when she hovered in the doorway of the place they appeared to call the Orchid Room. Drawn to it because it was partially lit by subtle lighting, Shona made her way through the tables to the darkest corner. Seating herself at an empty circular table, she watched the dancers moving to the music produced by a four-piece band.

A waiter approached, asking if she would prefer to wait for her partner to join her. 'I'm alone,' she answered, and ordered a drink, 'Nothing alcoholic. Orange juice?' The waiter nodded.

'With ice?' he asked.

'Better not,' she answered. 'I've been in bed most of the day and——'

The waiter made a sympathetic face. 'Another one? There's been a lot affected this time. Like a sandwich?'

'I'd love one. Something simple?'

The waiter nodded and went on his way.

Shona watched the dancers, their faces hardly distinguishable through the gloom. Many of the women wore evening dress, the men likewise. There was an intimate atmosphere about the place, romance if you felt romantic, glitter as a woman's ring or necklace caught the lowered lighting. The glass of orange juice accompanied by two sandwiches was placed in front of her. Shona paid the waiter, thanking him. As her teeth sank into the moist bread, she realised how hungry she was. It did not take her long to finish the sandwiches. With the food, some of her energy seemed to return.

As the last of the group of dances finished, the lights were turned higher. Some were blue, others gold, some a red glow. People sat in groups or twos. Watching them Shona felt, for the first time, lonely and out of place. Maybe she should have followed Marsh's advice and gone to bed. Her eyes roamed as the band rested and her gaze was caught by the sight of two people sitting, heads close, across the room next to the dance area and near to the band.

It took her only a few seconds to recognise Calvin's profile. It took about as long for her brain to tell her that his companion was Toni Hardy. The music began again, the lights were lowered and Calvin led his partner on to the dance floor. A young man with fair hair took up his position at the microphone. He sang a romantic song and its effect was noticeable on the moving couples. It was not only Calvin and Toni who had drawn closer together, Shona told herself determinedly. All the others had, too.

From her secret corner, Shona watched her fiancé with his new-found, even if strictly temporary, girl-friend. She had never seen Calvin so animated, except when rehearsing among his friends and exchanging with them musical jokes and whimsically misplayed harmonies.

As the two of them danced, looking with laughing interest into each other's faces, Shona saw again the uncharacteristic behaviour which Calvin had displayed when he had brought the tray to her cabin. He had been happy then, she had thought, at having discovered a substitute pianist for his evening concert. Watching them, it was not difficult to see that Toni's ability to accompany him on the piano was not the only reason for his out-of-character lightheartedness.

As the singer ended his song, the dance finished. The singer merged into the background, another dance began. Shona thought, when my orange juice is finished, I'll go back to my cabin.

'Disobeying my instructions?' The voice was familiar and heart-tugging, the tone too smooth to be trusted.

Her pulse-beat labouring painfully told Shona that he was probably right to question her presence there at such a late hour. The quick recovery from her earlier troubles had been more of an illusion than reality. As he drew out a chair and occupied it, she answered spiritedly,

'They weren't your instructions, they were the doctor's.' His elegantly covered shoulders lifted. 'His instructions, mine—it makes no difference. Why are you here?'

His dark, rather wayward hair, his formal jacket and tie, his eyes which glinted like the diamonds which had caught

the lighting were both daunting and a challenge. She refused to be intimidated by his position in the company's
hierarchy.

'I was bored, I had to get out of the cabin. I may be on
the cruise to work, but it's almost certainly the only vacation I'll have this year. Why should I spend so many
precious hours sleeping?'

'Then why,' the glinting eyes were half hidden by
lowered lids, 'spend so many precious moments in hiding.'
His hand caught her wrist and he pulled her to her feet.

'No, no. Please, Marsh, I don't think I'm quite strong
enough yet to be able to dance. Tomorrow, maybe,
but——'

She was being pulled behind him and as they reached
the dance floor, the lights were lowered again. 'If your legs
give way,' Marsh said in her ear over the noise of the band,
'just cling to me. No one would notice. Look around you
and you'll find at least half the couples dancing in close
physical contact, including,' his head turned slightly, 'your
loving fiancé.'

Her eyes swept the dance area, finding Calvin and Toni.
She had not realised before how professionally Calvin
danced. It was all connected, she guessed—music, harmony,
rhythm ... It came to her that not once since she had
known Calvin from their college days had they ever danced
together.

'What are you thinking?' Marsh had pulled her just a
little closer and his voice was soft, almost intimate, but she
did not mind. In the dreamlike state which had seemed
to take hold of her, she found the swaying of the ship no
longer frightening but soothing, the fanning of this man's
breath against her cheek exciting rather than a liberty, the
skim of lips over her temple deeply stirring, instead
of—— She could not tell him her thoughts, so she tried a
half-truth.

She smiled, seeking his eyes. 'That it's strange learning
that my fiancé can dance while I'm dancing in another
man's arms.' The arms of that 'other man' grew even

tighter. She stared at Marsh's shoulder. 'Has he seen me yet, do you think?'

'I doubt it. He seems too absorbed in the little baggage he's dancing with.' Marsh looked down at the stiffly held dark head. 'Do you want to hide from him?'

The eyes that found his were defiant. 'No, I don't! Why should I? If he feels he's free to do—what he's doing, then I'm free, too.'

'Well said, Miss Shona Carroll.' His eyes gleamed with amusement. 'Which means that I can look at *you* like a sick dog just as he's looking at her. I can nuzzle up to you,' his lips found her neck, 'hold you like this,' his hands went to her hips so that they were in hard contact with his, 'even kiss you if I feel the urge.'

'Stop it,' Shona whispered anxiously, 'other people are looking. That woman—that blonde over there——'

His lips hovered over hers. 'Who happens to be my mother,' he said casually.

Shona fought to prise herself from his hold. 'Why didn't you tell me? What will she think of me, seeing us like this?'

'It matters more to you what my mother thinks than what your fiancé thinks?'

'I didn't mean it that way.' She was growing agitated now as Marsh showed no indication of being ready to let her go. 'And Marsh—I'm feeling tired now.'

'You won't get away from me that way. Think of a better excuse. Until this moment you've shown every sign of being fit enough to dance all night.'

She shook her head violently and looked up at him, pleading, 'I want to go back to my seat.'

He must have seen her pale cheeks and decided to relent. Instead of returning her to her table, he held her arm and urged her to his own. Besides his mother there was an officer of senior rank at the table with a woman seated beside him, who, Shona assumed, was his wife.

'I've seen your photograph somewhere,' the officer began, studying Shona with bemused eyes. 'I never forget a pretty face.'

'What an original opening!' Verity commented, laughing. 'And in front of your wife, too. By the way,' she added, inviting Shona to sit beside her while her son sought another chair, 'may I introduce Peter and Yvonne Carmichael. Peter's the Chief Officer.'

Marsh took his place next to Shona. 'Peter, Yvonne,' he took up the introductions, 'this is Shona Carroll.'

'And you're right about my photograph,' Shona told them. 'It's in the glass display case with the other entertainers on board ship. I'm a pianist.'

'Strictly classical,' Marsh amplified, with a twisted smile. 'None of your pop or rock or whatever.'

Shona shot him a crushing glance, but he merely smiled broadly. 'You'd be surprised what I can tackle.'

'Would I now?' he asked goadingly. 'Could you tackle, say, a six-foot-three strong-armed male who assaulted you in a dark corner?'

'You're making the girl blush,' said Yvonne Carmichael, lifting a glass to her lips.

'That's nothing to what he was doing to her on the dance floor,' Verity commented, smiling. 'Did I forget to warn you about my son and women, Shona?'

'You warned me, thanks,' replied Shona. 'I'll remember the warning,' with a flashing smile at the man of whom they were talking, 'until the end of the cruise us do part.'

She continued smiling in spite of the coldness in Marsh Faraday's eyes, keeping tightly to herself the secret which her own mind had just revealed to her—that, even after knowing this man for less than two days, she was already dreading their eventual parting.

Verity asked if she felt better now, and Shona said, 'Yes, thank you.' To Peter Carmichael Verity said, 'The force eight gale got her.'

Peter nodded. 'It went through over half the passengers and about thirty per cent of the crew like a knife through butter. We had to postpone the Captain's cocktail party, otherwise there would have been nobody there—except the Captain!'

'So I didn't miss it?' Shona asked happily.

'It's tomorrow evening,' Verity told her.

'So you didn't bring your most expensive evening dress for nothing,' was Marsh's sardonic comment.

'I thought you were ill in bed.' Calvin was beside her. Toni stood next to him.

Verity laughed. 'You look disappointed to see her, and you her fiancé, too!'

Calvin had the grace to look uncomfortable.

'She's had a ringside view of you making the *close* acquaintance of one of the ship's best-known man-traps,' Marsh said, a malicious gleam in his eyes.

'We were just talking,' Calvin said defensively. 'Weren't we, Toni?'

The girl caught his hand. 'You didn't tell me you were engaged, Cal.'

Shona shivered at the name. Surely he'd slap her down for shortening his name as he did everyone else?

'Thought you knew,' he said, affecting a careless attitude and to Shona's astonishment uttering not one word of reproof about his abbreviated name.

'Glad to hear it, since Toni's supposed to be my girl.' All heads turned at the words. The young man who had sung with the band stood there, shoulders pushed forward, hands in pockets.

'Danny, whoever told you that?' Toni exclaimed, her face in the subdued lighting an angry red.

'What would you call yourself, then?' Danny retorted. 'Any man's woman?'

Toni made a sharp movement but checked herself. She would, Shona was certain, have slapped the young man's face if they hadn't been in such elevated company.

Danny's eyes rested with interest on Shona. 'Introduce me, Toni.' To Shona, 'Haven't I seen you somewhere before?'

There was laughter. 'Full circle,' Yvonne Carmichael commented dryly. 'You've just stolen my husband's line. Actually, her photograph is in the same place as yours—

plus all the other entertainers on this particular cruise.'

'In the display case in the office foyer,' her husband explained.

Danny came round to Shona's other side. 'So what's your line—singing, dancing?'

'Piano playing,' Toni told him, 'which she does a darned sight better than I do. She's Calvin's partner.' To Shona, 'I made a real mess of the concert this evening, didn't I, Cal?'

Calvin looked embarrassed and rubbed his ear. 'In view of the short notice, it wasn't too bad at all.'

If that had been me, Shona thought angrily, he'd have torn me to pieces for letting him down.

'You're right, Miss Hardy.' Marsh spoke at last, and his words were candid. 'You did come very near to making a mess of the concert.' She nodded as Marsh went on, with equal candour, 'But Mr Faber's such a brilliant flautist, I think he covered quite satisfactorily the mistakes you made.' Calvin mopped his forehead, not knowing where to look. Satisfied with the effect his reducing tactics were having on the flute player, Marsh continued, 'I'm looking forward with great anticipation to hearing the expert accompanist again tomorrow evening.'

'Making sure, by jogging my conscience, that I won't renege on the contract, Mr Faraday?'

His narrowed eyes met hers. 'If you did that, Miss Carroll,' he returned blandly, 'you wouldn't be the only one to suffer loss of income. Your fiancé would, too.'

'Shona, be quiet!' Calvin snapped, lowering his voice. 'You know very well you'll be playing tomorrow evening.' He tugged at Toni's arm. 'Come on, let's dance.'

Toni raised a hand to the group, gave Danny a scornful look and followed Calvin. As if in retaliation, Danny turned quickly to Shona. 'Like to dance?'

Shona had been about to leave but, knowing exactly how the young man felt about being abandoned by the girl he seemed to care for, agreed. Excusing herself from the others and giving Marsh a swift, rebellious look, she joined

Danny, moving to the music, thankful that it was slow and relaxing.

'So you're a pianist,' said Danny, looking at her with interest. 'Strictly classical? Contemptuous of everything written after the last century?'

'Musically, I have very wide tastes. From the purely traditional to the very modern. Even your kind of stuff.' She smiled into his interested eyes which were level with hers. 'When I say modern, I mean it—pieces where you almost have to get inside the piano to play the notes. You know, lean right over and pluck the strings, and so on.'

'You can't mean it?' When she nodded he shook his head in mock disbelief. 'And there we are, us groups and break-away groups, thinking we're the very latest in musical sounds. Looks like we've been so wrong.'

Shona laughed. 'I like your singing,' she said.

'Truly? Thanks a lot. I value your opinion. Look,' he glanced around for about the fourth time since the dance had started, and found Toni talking animatedly to Calvin, 'how about us, you and me, getting together some time and playing something? Making it up as we go, if you like? I play the guitar as well as sing. I could do my stuff, maybe you could improvise, see what it sounds like.'

'Something like an experiment? Sounds fine to me. I'm interested in anything new.'

He looked at her. 'Even a new man?'

Her eyes dropped. 'Sorry, Danny.'

'Okay. Guess I'm just mad at Toni.'

Shona knew that was her cue to say, 'And me about Calvin,' but the words would not come.

CHAPTER FOUR

It was at breakfast next morning that Shona saw Marsh again. As she and Calvin joined him, they found that his mother was absent.

'She's being lazy this morning,' Marsh explained. 'She's ordered a Continental breakfast to be served in her cabin.'

Shona smiled. 'I must try that some time.'

'You're here to work,' said Calvin. 'Isn't that so, Mr Faraday?'

Shona noticed that Marsh did not invite Calvin to drop the surname. 'That is so,' Marsh agreed, eyeing Shona lazily. 'However, I think the shipping company will permit your fiancée to relax occasionally. Not very often, of course.' His eyelids lowered as he took in her freshness, her invitingly feminine shape. 'Just enough to keep her fit so that she can fulfil that contract.'

Shona saw the mockery in his eyes and said between her teeth, 'There are times, Mr Faraday, when I'd like to do that——' she made a tearing motion with her hands, 'to the contract.'

'Then, Miss Carroll,' was his instant reply, 'you'd find yourself paying a large amount of money to the shipping company for the cruise you're taking—at the moment at their expense.'

Colour sweeping over her cheeks enhanced her attractiveness, although she was unaware of its effect. Marsh said, appearing pleased with himself, 'You're looking a great deal better this morning, Shona.'

Calvin's head moved jerkily from his fiancée to the man who had addressed her by her first name. He frowned at what he seemed to think was a liberty, but he stayed silent, returning to studying the menu.

Noting Calvin's displeasure and smiling to herself, Shona

answered, 'I'm feeling much better, Marsh, thank you.'

Marsh smiled at his menu. Shona looked with a smug satisfaction at hers. As they were eating, Marsh said, 'We arrive at Vigo today. We dock,' he consulted his watch, 'in an hour and a half. Will you go ashore, Shona?'

She saw, glancing quickly at Calvin, that he was turning an angry red. 'I think I might, Marsh,' she answered brightly.

'I've drawn up a schedule of work for today,' Calvin snapped. 'It precludes going ashore. I'm sorry.'

Shona's lightweight conversation with Marsh Faraday had been a cover. Underneath, she was angry—with Calvin, with the unpleasant tone he adopted when talking to her, with his failure to discuss matters with her instead of issuing orders. Most of all, she still had not forgiven him for the casual way he had temporarily ended their engagement.

The fact that he still had power to hurt her was also a source of annoyance. It could mean only one thing, she supposed—that she loved him in spite of his shortcomings. Her feelings for him had, since she had first heard him perform, even at music college, been spiced with a kind of reverence. So what did she truly feel for him, love or hero-worship?

It was not, she told herself firmly, the time for deep self-analysis. After an ascetic day yesterday as a result of her malady, her appetite was in dire need of appeasing. Energetically she tackled the food she had ordered, bringing a smile to Marsh's face.

Munching her buttered and honeyed toast and eating the poached egg and sausage, she said defensively, 'I'm hungry.'

Marsh laughed. 'If ever two words were unnecessary, they were.'

'I'm sorry. In future, I'll edit all my sentences so that they're more pleasing to your ear.'

'Starving your body seems to have sharpened your wit.' Marsh's words were clipped, his eyes cool.

Calvin asked, pouring himself coffee and filling Shona's

cup, too, 'Are you going ashore, Mr Faraday?'

'This morning,' Marsh replied. 'I'm walking round the town with my mother. At Vigo, the ship takes on supplies. Often they're brought here all the way from Britain.'

'You mean by air?' Shona asked, surprised.

Marsh laughed. 'No. Across the channel by ferry in containers. Then they're driven south through France and Spain, mainly by British truck drivers.'

Calvin was as surprised as Shona. 'Doesn't that greatly add to the cost?'

'Oddly,' Marsh answered, 'it actually saves money, in view of the fact that handling charges at Southampton Docks at present work out to be higher than the transport of the goods across Europe.' He pushed back his chair. 'If you'll excuse me ... I must find my mother.' He flicked a smile at Shona. 'Enjoy your piano practice. And remember, it's what we're paying you for.' His grin and hand raised in mock-protection inflamed Shona's anger even more.

With Calvin leading the way, Shona left the restaurant. As they climbed the stairs instead of waiting for the lift, Calvin said he would see her in her cabin in fifteen minutes. He left her gazing in the window of one of the shops on board which, since the ship was nearing port was not opening that day until evening.

Glancing round the corner, she saw that Calvin had disappeared. All the time people were coming and going through the double swing doors which led to the promenade deck. Telling herself she would only be five minutes, she joined the line of people who were on their way out. Since there was a strong breeze, they were wearing jackets and sweaters.

It seemed the docking of the ship would be early since the port was near enough to see the place in detail. Tugs attached to lines were easing the ship towards its berth. Shona noticed for the first time that the throbbing to which she had grown accustomed beneath her feet had stopped. Together with many others, she leaned on the rail to watch the ship's docking.

It was only when she looked around her and noted the other passengers' almost mesmerised interest in the proceedings that she remembered the time limit she had set on her own diversion from her real destination. Ten minutes had passed, her watch informed her, instead of five.

She turned and pushed her way through the crowds, shouldering herself through the swing doors and racing across to the stairs. The lift would take too long to come, as she had learned by experience. In her headlong race to be at her cabin on time, she weaved her way between the tall and the short, the thin and the plump, going headlong into a person who materialised as being male.

After prising herself from his body, her eyes lifted to meet those of the man who seemed to be wherever she went. As she apologised, pushing back her ruffled hair, his raised eyebrows taunted. 'Playing truant, Miss Carroll? That will never do. If you're not quick, you'll be getting the rough side of your fiancé's tongue.'

Marsh Faraday's hands held her elbows and she stood where he had put her—within touching distance of his hard, lean frame. At that moment she did not particularly care about the haranguing which would come her way for keeping her fiancé waiting. She didn't care very much about anything—apart from the feelings which Marsh's proximity and hold were arousing in her. Dismayed that even the disinterested touch of him could throw her emotions so off-balance, she twisted away and continued to battle her way to her destination.

Shona and Calvin were alone for lunch. Marsh and his mother seemed to have decided to stay ashore. Calvin talked music. Shona listened interestedly at first, but her attention soon began to wander. It was a long time before she gave up straining to look for Marsh. She wondered whether she would see him again that day.

The afternoon was warmer. Either the wind had dropped or it might have been, Shona reasoned, that they were sheltered by the great bay in which the port of Vigo was situated. Passengers who had stayed aboard—others had left the ship for tours arranged by the shipping company—were relaxing in deck chairs and sunloungers. Shona experienced a sudden wish to join them.

As they walked up the flights of stairs to their cabins, Calvin must have seen her eyes straying to the exits as they passed them. 'We can't join the passengers,' he told her. 'You need practice after your day off yesterday, and we need to rehearse that music we looked through this morning. I think it's a reasonable mixture of light classical and popular. Some of it should have the elderly ladies plunging back to their youth.'

Shona disliked the touch of scorn in his voice as he spoke. One day, she thought, you'll be old and then—— It struck her that she had not, at that moment, imagined herself growing old with him—which was strange, considering they were engaged to be married.

Calvin collected his instrument from the cabin, while Shona took the pile of music they had chosen for performance that evening. They went up to the theatre, which was where they had practised before. The piano stood open and there was a microphone placed to one side. It would no doubt be used later that day when a special gala show had been promised by the regular entertainments staff.

As they sorted themselves out, someone called, 'Hi!' It was Danny Mercer, the singer with whom Shona had danced the night before. He came towards them, making for the microphone. 'Just remembered I forgot to disconnect this after we'd been rehearsing this morning.' He attended to it, then eyed them, surprised. 'What are you two up to? This isn't your home ground.'

'Rehearsing for this evening's classical concert,' Calvin told him irritably.

'So you want me to get the hell out of here.' Shona smiled at him sweetly, hoping to counter Calvin's sourness. Danny asked casually, 'Seen Toni anywhere?' The question was asked of Calvin, but addressed to Shona. She shook her head. Calvin pretended not to hear.

'Would she have gone ashore?' Shona offered.

'Yeah, probably with a member of the crew. Male, of course,' he added in disgust at his girl-friend's apparently habitual desertion of him. 'I ought to give that bitch up, before she gives me the brush-off. Sorry,' he apologised to Shona, 'but I'm in a foul mood. Hey, don't forget my suggestion that we might get together and work out something.'

Calvin looked up suspiciously. 'Work out what?'

Danny looked at Shona, who answered, 'Oh, something.' Calvin scowled, Danny smiled and walked away. Calvin asked, 'Ready, Shona?' She nodded and lifted her hands over the keys. The fluid notes of the flute floated outward, echoing round the empty hall. Shona played, gently, sweetly, fading her performance discreetly into the background as a good accompanist should.

Listening intently to Calvin's playing, she missed her cue and he jerked the flute from his lips. 'For heaven's sake, keep your mind on what you're doing. I won't have you messing up my performance through inattention.'

Shona swivelled on the stool. 'I was listening to you, Calvin. I was thinking——'

'I don't care what you were thinking. We're supposed to be playing together, not separately.' Shona turned back to the piano. Calvin sighed. 'Okay, let's start again.'

Shona felt resentment stir, then she forced herself to be reasonable, acknowledging that Calvin was right. Maybe she had not yet fully recovered from yesterday's trouble. They played another piece and again the exquisitely executed phrases which came from the instrument in Calvin's hands filled the emptiness in the hall.

After a third item of music, Calvin attended to his flute and said, keeping his eyes on it, 'Your playing is hardly of the kind to inspire a soloist to reach the heights of achievement. Can't you do better than that?'

Again Shona swivelled to face him. 'For goodness' sake, Calvin, I'm doing my best. I've got the same musical qualifications as you. What's wrong with my playing? I'm acting the self-effacing accompanist, aren't I? Or is it that in your opinion, I'm not self-effacing enough? Am I too good, so good in fact that there's a danger that I might overshadow you?'

Her bitter retaliation surprised Shona herself. She had never spoken to Calvin in such a way before. But, she rationalised, it's time I stopped being a doormat to Calvin. Maybe Marsh Faraday had been right when he had accused her of letting Calvin walk over her.

'Look,' Calvin answered, spite contorting his face, 'I've never told you before, but I think you're such a lousy pianist you make my skin crawl.' He grasped his flute with both hands and marched across the floor and out through the swing doors.

Just before he disappeared she shouted after him, 'Why, you miserable, pig-headed——!' He had gone. Her eyes jerked back to the piano, she lifted her hands and brought them down in an ear-splitting noise twice. Then she thought, I'll show everyone, myself included ... And she broke into the rousing, arresting, crashing chords of the start of Tchaikovsky's Piano Concerto Number One.

The notes rippled from her fingers, her body was gripped by a frenzy of music, her foot was pressed on the loud pedal. She was totally absorbed in making music in her way, pleasing herself instead of someone else, music of her own choice—until two hands came from behind her and gripped her wrists, forcing them upwards and sideways. There was a deafening silence.

Shona turned. 'What do you think you're——' It was Marsh Faraday and his anger had implanted storm signals in his eyes.

'Are you aware,' he said icily, 'that every note you've played, every word you've said, every bit of your petty quarrelling with your fiancé has been picked up by the microphone and broadcast up and down this deck, overheard by the unfortunate passengers who opted to remain on board this afternoon instead of going ashore?'

Shona twisted her wrists away and swirled the stool

round to face him. 'It can't have been,' she remonstrated. 'Danny Mercer came in saying he'd forgotten to disconnect it last night and did it while we sat here.'

'I'm sorry to have to inform you,' was the cold response, 'that Danny Mercer must have forgotten switching it off last night and this afternoon actually switched it *on*. I've now put matters right and you can no longer be overheard,' he added. Her face paled under his accusing gaze. 'The music you accidentally broadcast,' he went on caustically, 'was acceptable, even pleasant. The arguments were childish in the extreme and not to be tolerated from those employed by the management on board this ship.'

Shona stood, confronting him, but still, to her annoyance, having to look up to meet his eyes. 'Please accept my apologies. They'll be the only ones you'll get, because I know from experience that Calvin never apologises to anyone. Please also,' she endeavoured to hide the pleasure it was giving her to say the words, 'accept my withdrawal from the contract the shipping company made with Calvin Faber and his accompanist, Jake Watson.' Her eyes flashed. 'You see, I only came along for the ride!'

She made to go, but Marsh's hand came out, stopping her. 'You came in order to take the place of the indisposed accompanist.'

'I came out of the goodness of my heart, Mr Faraday. Unfortunately, my heart just isn't "good" any more.' She walked away, turned back. 'So you'll just have to find a replacement for me, won't you? If you're lucky, there may be a passenger who learnt to play the piano as a child, and can still thump out a note or two.' Her head high, she swung round again.

'In that case, I'd be obliged if you would go at once to the purser's office and pay over a large sum of money,' he named the amount, 'to cover the cost of your holiday cruise.' With a malicious smile he watched her flinch as she absorbed the three-figured amount into her mind.

Moistening her lips, she said, 'I—I hope he won't mind

if I give it to him in stages. Some now, some just after the cruise and the rest——'

He strolled towards her, hands in pockets.

'Since passengers pay their fares two months *ahead* of any cruise with this shipping company, I'm afraid that what you're suggesting isn't acceptable. The entire amount will have to be paid at once.'

'You can't mean it?' Her large eyes gazed into his.

'As a director of the company, Miss Carroll, I mean every word.' His eyes, cold as the sea had been yesterday, looked through her. 'Well, do you withdraw your withdrawal from the contract?'

She swallowed hard, fury turning her a deep pink, deepening the brown of her eyes. 'I haven't any choice, have I?' she countered. 'Money's a very powerful weapon, as you very well know. In fact, you seem obsessed by it.'

'On the company's behalf,' he said softly, 'not on my own.'

She made a disbelieving noise, then continued, 'Guessing, as you probably have by now, that I just don't have the kind of money that enables people to take luxury cruises like this, you're holding that weapon very effectively over my head. Or,' with heavy sarcasm, 'do I feel the touch of cold steel on my neck?'

His hand moved with lightning speed and gripped her throat. Now her throat was burning with the pressure of his fingers. She choked, 'If you throttle me, Mr Faraday, you'll *have* to find another pianist, won't you?' His hold tightened and she grew afraid. 'If—if you don't let go, there'll be bruise marks on my neck. Then what would the audience say when I perform in front of them?'

As he released her, his hand moved—deliberately, she was sure—upwards against her chin, knocking her backwards until she staggered to keep her balance.

Anger burned in her eyes and she tried to express it in words, but nothing would come. Somehow tears had blocked her speech processes. She turned and ran, making for the swing doors, racing down the stairs which took her to the deck from which passengers were disembarking. Slowing down, she joined the line for the door which led to the gangway.

At the door she was handed a re-boarding ticket and told to retain it for use during the rest of the cruise. Nodding, she made her way carefully down the sloping gangway and found herself for the first time on Spanish soil. Having no knowledge of what to do, she followed the other passengers. It was then she realised she had left her passport in her cabin, but she refused to turn back for fear of bumping into Marsh Faraday.

Walking up the steps after the others, she found herself in an ornate Customs hall. The place echoed with talk and laughter. There were two or three Customs officers lounging around, eyes alert but merely lingering. Going down the steps which led out of the graceful building, she walked to some open gates. There, police stood. Shona approached one, saying, 'My passport——' but he motioned her on.

To her right was a row of souvenir shops and the area was filled with tourists. It was like a magnet which, like so many others, she could not resist. She gazed at display boxes, shelf extensions outside the shops which held leather bags and purses and belts. There were rotating stands displaying cards bearing attractive photographs of the area. She peeped in the shop windows, her gaze lingering on the steelware, the necklaces and rings.

In one shop window there was a display of Spanish dolls. Their dresses were dazzlingly bright, their attitudes those of dancers. They were of many sizes, some large, others small enough to hold in the hand. Taking courage from seeing other passengers in the shop, Shona entered and looked around. An assistant came forward and asked in accented English if he could help her.

'Those dolls,' said Shona, gesturing, 'the ones in the window.'

Which colour? she was asked, and answered that she was not sure. The young man found a long pole with a hook at the end and said, encouragingly, 'You tell me the one.'

Shona gazed long and hard at the back views of the dolls in the window, trying to decide on the size and colour of the dresses. Pointing to one in purple and white, she watched as the assistant hooked the doll and brought it down.

Inspecting it admiringly, Shona asked the price. When he told her how many pesetas would be needed to pay for it, she shook her head sorrowfully and asked to see another, smaller doll. This also he managed to remove from the window display. The colour of its dress was not as striking as her first choice but since it was smaller, she knew it would not be so expensive.

This proved to be the case, but she picked up the other doll again, sighing that price put it beyond her reach. Eventually she told him she would take the smaller doll and the young man nodded, wrapping it carefully. When his voice prodded her gently, naming the pesetas she would need to give him, Shona returned from her dreaming and turned to find her purse—only to remember that, in her precipitate departure from the ship, she had left it behind.

A shaking hand went to her head. For a moment, she had thought she had lost her bag and everything it contained. All the same, it meant that she would not be able to pay for the doll.

'Could you put it aside for me?' she asked. 'I've left my money on the ship. It won't take me long to——' She stopped, remembering that if she spent precious moments going all the way back to her cabin and coming back here, there would be no time for her to look round the town, since the ship was due to sail in a little over an hour.

Sadly she shook her head. 'Never mind, I'll have to leave it.' With a sweet yet unhappy smile, she apologised for wasting the young man's time and went slowly to the door. Her head was down, her thoughts were with the doll she had so nearly bought. Her body came up against a tall, solid male figure which filled the doorway.

Marsh Faraday's arms went round her and she found herself gazing up into his mocking eyes. 'You just can't do anything right today, can you?' he taunted. 'Playing wrong notes, broadcasting your disagreement with your fiancé to an intrigued if surprised audience. And now leaving your money behind. What shall I do with you?'

'Let me go, that's what you can do,' she parried, and squeezed past him. To her surprise and slightly to her chagrin, he did let her go. She continued walking, away from the ship and towards the town. There were stone-coloured buildings, tall and twentieth-century in design.

Arriving at the side of a busy double highway, she paused. Sensing she was not alone, she glanced side-ways and saw Marsh watching the fast-moving traffic and waiting for a space large enough to allow him to cross. When she felt his hand grasp her arm and urge her across with him, she pulled away indignantly.

'Unless you want us both run down,' he said tightly, eyes going swiftly from right to left and back again, 'I'd advise you to behave like a responsible adult instead of a rebellious child.'

Closing her mouth tightly, she allowed his guiding hand to remain until they had negotiated the other highway. As they made their way through the hurrying inhabitants and strolling tourists, passing groups of lounging young people, Shona asked, 'Where are we going?'

She had said 'we'! Noticing her slip at once, Marsh smiled. '*We* are going to the park over there. We can't stay long. The ship sails soon.'

In the park, Marsh pulled her to sit beside him on a bench. At a fountain nearby some young men were push-ing and fooling in an effort to unbalance their friends. Some were in the water and, disregarding their soaked clothes, were splashing the others and laughing loudly. Palm trees grew high and the sun threw patterns on to the ground, speckling it with light and shadow.

'Marsh?' His name came from her shyly. His head

turned slowly and he appeared to have been deep in thought. 'You said you're one of the directors.' He nodded. 'What's your particular line?'

'I'm the chief executive of one of Ocean Rover's subsidiaries, an engineering company.' He mentioned a well known name. 'Apart from our contracts with a number of countries overseas, one of our divisions services Ocean Rover's fleet of cruise ships.'

'Oh.' The reply was spoken in a small voice.

It must have amused him because he said, with a smile, 'Do you now realise the high status of the man who's taken the trouble to escort you round the town?' Her eyes sought his as if unsure about the sincerity of his words. Then she saw his smile and retorted,

'Oh, yes, Mr Faraday.' She spoke with a mock breathlessness. 'I now know what a lucky girl I am to have as my companion a man who occupies such an elevated position in Ocean Rover Shipping Company. I look on him with real awe.'

His smile broadened. He rose, drawing her up and forgetting, it seemed, to release her hand. They walked, thus linked, back to the road, crossing it carefully and making for the ship.

'It's a pleasant place,' said Shona, to make conversation, since Marsh seemed to have become preoccupied again. Their hands were still linked and the nerves in Shona's hand and arm appeared to have grown exquisitely sensitive.

'Vigo?' Marsh replied. 'The town has grown a great deal over the years. The bay is twenty miles long and three miles wide. The water is very deep, too.' They were approaching the line of tourists' shops. 'It's said that the bay is large enough to hold the combined fleets of the world.'

Shona was impressed and would have been more so had they not at that moment been passing the shop in which she had so nearly bought the Spanish dancing doll. Her eyes slid secretly to the window, but she could not see the doll.

'Why are you sighing?'

The question surprised her since she had not been aware of doing so. 'The doll I wanted,' she said. 'I can't see it. Either they haven't got around to putting it back in the window or it's been sold.'

'Things like that go fast when the cruise ships dock here. Passengers descend like locusts, like——' he lifted their linked hands, 'this one who's clinging on to me for dear life.'

Annoyed at his deliberate reversal of the facts, she tried to jerk her fingers free.

He held them effortlessly, however, and if anything, more tightly. 'Except,' he went on, 'that none of them forgets to bring their money with them when they go shopping.'

Now they were walking through the echoing Customs hall, walking down the steps and along the quay towards the gangway. Something made Shona lift her head and gaze at the ship. Calvin was leaning against the rail on the Promenade Deck, watching them. At once a feeling of guilt crept over Shona and she tried to shake off Marsh's hand.

Marsh glanced at her, frowning, followed her eyes then smiled to himself. While his attention was momentarily distracted, Shona managed to free her hand. She hurried up the gangway, pausing to show the embarkation card which she had pushed into a pocket.

'Thank you for showing me the town, Marsh,' she said, turning.

'I could have shown you a great deal more, if there'd been time.'

His eyes held an almost friendly expression. They exchanged smiles which upturned Shona's heart. 'You look,' she ventured, 'as if you might even manage to like me if you tried.'

Now there was a narrow look about him. 'Is that an invitation?' Shona was puzzled. 'I never guessed you were that kind of girl,' he added, his gaze lowering and seeking out every part of her femininity which her button-through sundress revealed.

Shona felt foolishly as if she wanted to wrap her arms about her, keeping out his raking eyes. 'If you want to know,' she returned acidly, 'I was being sarcastic. You're so aloof and on your dignity I doubt if you could *like* any woman.' Passengers were coming and going all the time. Shona added in a low voice, 'Make love to them, maybe, but not because you *like* them, only for the fun of it.'

His flicker of a smile preceded his question, 'So you think I could, if I tried very hard, like you as well as making love to you? Mm,' he pretended to consider, 'it's worth a try.' With a gleam, 'Name the hour, Miss Carroll.'

'You're deliberately twisting my words again!' With which accusation she swung round to go.

'See you at the Captain's cocktail party,' he called, 'in approximately one hour's time.'

'I'll do my best,' she answered over her shoulder, 'not to see you!'

Calvin was waiting outside her cabin. 'Where have you been?' His tone was, as usual, irritable.

'Shopping.' She opened her cabin door with the key from her pocket. 'Except that I forgot to take any money. I—er—left the ship in rather a hurry.'

He did not ask why. 'You seem very friendly with Marsh Faraday.'

'Well?' She opened the cosmetics compartment and sat on the stool. 'I might say that you seem very friendly with Toni Hardy, Which means we're quits, doesn't it?'

He shrugged. 'A chance friendship on a cruise. What's nine or ten days? Nothing can develop in that short time.'

'By nothing, I imagine you mean a relationship?' Shona was combing her hair. 'You'd be surprised,' she sounded far more worldly than she had intended, but did not care, 'how a relationship can develop in one evening.' She added wickedly, 'After all, there's always the long night to follow, isn't there?'

'What's happened to you?' he demanded. 'What have you been up to?'

'Tut tut, Calvin. Don't you trust your fiancée? Oh, sorry, our engagement's non-existent while we're on board, isn't it?'

'I know what's wrong,' said Calvin, without, Shona noticed, correcting her statement about the suspension of their engagement, 'you're jealous!'

She swung round on the stool, comb poised. 'I'm most certainly not.' To her immense surprise she found that once again, she meant it. There was an exhilaration inside her that could not be explained. It had nothing whatsoever to do with Calvin's presence in her cabin. To his reflection she said, 'Would you mind going now? I'd like to change for the cocktail party.'

'Hell, I'd forgotten.' He quoted, 'The Captain requests the pleasure . . .' At the door he said, 'I'll go and dress up. Remember the concert we're giving.'

She smiled at her own reflection. 'Are you warning me not to drink too much at the Captain's party?'

A slam of the door was her answer.

The engines were throbbing and the ship was away under her own steam by the time Shona was ready to go with Calvin to the Captain's cocktail party.

Before calling on Calvin in his cabin, she paused before the long mirror. Her dress was one she had worn on the few occasions on which she had performed as piano soloist with orchestras in the north-west of England. Her cabin steward had pressed the dress and now it looked as fresh as if she had just bought it.

It was long-sleeved, and fell with a slight flare to her ankles. The neckline encircled her throat and the top of the dress hugged her shape, fastening with tiny buttons from the inward-curving waistline to the very top. The pattern was bronzed leaves on a white background. Her only jewellery was gilt earrings. Her hair, with its centre parting, framed her face.

Would Calvin praise her appearance when he let her into his cabin? She found she would have to wait to know his reaction since once again her tapping on the door elicited no response. He couldn't, she thought, he could not have gone without me! It seemed he had indeed gone to the Captain's party without her, without even telling her, either.

Incensed, she walked swiftly to the stairs. Outside the Equator Room there was a constantly increasing mass of people. The women wore evening dresses revealing arms and shoulders which had not yet begun to show signs of tan from the sun's warmth. The men were as formally attired as their women partners. Looking at the couples, Shona felt suddenly alone and forsaken.

It was then that she saw Calvin talking to a girl with blonde hair and smiling face. He had left his fiancée to fend for herself and was contemplating escorting Toni Hardy to the Captain's cocktail party? Or was it Toni who was escorting him?

What did it matter? It did not alter the fact that Calvin was treating her, his fiancée, abominably, shedding her not only from his responsibility but from his mind. But was she really his fiancée? Shouldn't she feel as free as he plainly did and seek another escort? Her eyes searched the groups of people who were standing around. If only Danny Mercer was somewhere to be seen ...

As her eyes searched desperately for him, she found herself looking straight at Verity Faraday. In two seconds Shona came to a decision and pushed her way through the tightly-packed crowds. Anyone, she thought, rather than be alone, and who better than Mrs Faraday to help to put her at her ease? It had not occurred to her to try to discover whether her arrogant son was with her.

He was there behind his mother, deep in discussion with another passenger. Pausing in his conversation, Marsh looked expressionlessly at Shona. It was as though he didn't even know her! she thought indignantly. Then she recalled her final words to him as they parted after their walk round Vigo. '*I'll do my best,*' she'd said, '*not to see you!*' It seemed that he was taking immense pleasure in turning the tables on her.

'Shona dear,' said Verity, who looked magnificent in a draped rose pink gown, and whose blonde hair was dressed high, 'you're surely not alone?' Shona nodded, managing a smile.

'Mind if I go in with you, Mrs Faraday?'

'Marsh and I would be delighted,' she said, her voice rising over the chatter, 'wouldn't we, Marsh?'

Marsh either pretended not to hear or was too immersed in his discussion. Whatever it was, he showed no signs of responding. Undaunted, his mother called even louder. 'Marsh!' he turned at last, but slowly, 'Shona is alone.' She mouthed the words as if he could lip-read. 'She wants you to escort her in.' Her hand waved towards the Equator Room.

'No, no,' Shona denied, and shook her head vigorously, 'it was your mother's idea, not mine. I'll find my fiancé— I mean, Calvin——'

'Make up your mind.' Marsh was standing beside his mother now. His smile, as he looked down at Shona, could hardly be described as encouraging. He glanced over people's heads and commented, 'I imagine your *fiancé* would hardly take kindly to being snatched from his present partner at this particular moment.'

The voice of one of the officers rang out, 'Miss Toni Hardy and Mr Calvin Faber.' The crowd moved forward and Shona found herself propelled towards the entrance to the room.

'Found your fiancé, Miss Carroll?' Marsh asked sarcastically. He was beside her now. Behind them was his mother.

Shona turned, saying, 'Mrs Faraday, you can't go in alone. Marsh would rather be your escort than mine. I— I've changed my mind. I won't go to the cocktail party after all.' She started to battle against the thrust of people. Arms, hands and legs began to grow annoyed with her. A hand came out and grabbed her arm, hauling her back, forcing her to turn round and resume her place at his side.

'Will you behave?' Marsh muttered. 'My mother's found herself an escort.'

Shona, fighting to remove the iron grip from her arm, turned yet again and saw Mrs Faraday waving. 'John, over here. I'm partnerless. Would you be a dear——?'

The man called John was grey-haired and pink-cheeked and seemed only too pleased to accept the invitation. 'He's such a dear,' Verity confided to Shona. 'He's a widower and alone in life like me. John Victor, Shona Carroll, our lovely pianist. You know my son, of course.'

The introductions over, Shona discovered that they were near enough to the entrance to see the Captain's hand coming out to greet each new set of guests. Then it was her turn, hers and Marsh's. He bent and murmured in the officer's ear and she heard her name. 'Don't mention me,' Shona heard Marsh whisper. 'The Captain knows me almost as well as you know me. Okay?'

'Miss Shona Carroll.' Shona nearly jumped when her name echoed round the room. Marsh's arm rested round her waist as she placed her hand in the Captain's. He smiled his smile, lifted his hand in a friendly salute to Marsh, then Shona felt herself being urged on.

Marsh caught the attention of a steward and a tray was carried towards them. A drink was placed in her hand, a plate in the other. The ship rolled, reminding the chattering, laughing passengers that once again they were on the open sea.

At the movement, Shona gasped softly. 'Marsh,' she whispered, almost as a plea, 'it's surely not going to start again?'

He smiled and ran a finger down her cheek from which the colour had already begun to drain. 'It may be a bit rough at first, but don't worry,' he reassured, 'it'll be nothing like as bad as last time. I checked with the bridge—wind speed, weather conditions ahead, sea swell and so on.'

The relief showed in her face.

'What are you looking so happy about?' asked Verity, joining them glass in hand, her escort, John, not far behind. 'My dear, your plate's empty. Marsh, are you starving this girl?'

'Yes,' replied her son, the look in his eyes disturbing, 'into submission.'

His mother laughed and John looked at Marsh knowingly. 'That's one way,' he commented.

At Mrs Faraday's request, a steward brought a tray of food and Shona selected two small sandwiches and a canapé. A laugh rang out close by and Shona's head turned. Together with Mrs Faraday, she watched Calvin as he recovered from a joke which Toni had told him. They were in a group of people who were, Shona recognised, some of the ship's entertainments crew. She had never seen Calvin so animated.

Verity Faraday said, 'I see your fiancé's enjoying himself, Shona.'

Turning her back on him, Shona answered, 'I am, too.' Gazing up at Marsh, she added, 'Very much.' There was a note in her voice which might, by an astute listener, have been interpreted as defiance, and there was no doubt at all that Marsh Faraday was indeed astute.

He bent down and whispered in her ear, 'Jealous?'

Furious at his shrewdness, she hissed back, eyes flashing, 'No!'

'No?' Were his brows arched in mockery or sincerity? 'You should be.'

Knowing no other way of dampening down her sudden urge to throw the contents of her glass in his face—hadn't he spoken the truth, and wasn't the truth something which at this moment she didn't want to think about?—she threw the alcohol down her throat instead.

The coughing fit that followed made Marsh laugh as Calvin had laughed, and it was Verity's escort, John, who relieved her of her empty glass and patted her on the back. Verity scolded her son who, although still laughing, came to her aid by offering his handkerchief.

Shona shook her head hard, once. With a long-suffering sigh, he handed his mother his drink and bent down himself to dry her tears.

'Is this what you wanted?' he murmured under cover of the other passengers' chatter, the level of which was becoming deafening. 'Am I helping you to revenge yourself on your fiancé by showing you the attention he's showing to the blonde at his side?' He put his handkerchief away and retrieved his glass from his mother. She waved to a friend and took her willing, uncomplaining escort with her.

Shona picked up a sandwich and bit into it. Coinciding disconcertingly with the choking fit there had occurred inside her mind a small explosion. Her reaction to Calvin's behaviour had not, as Marsh suggested, been sparked off by jealousy or envy. It had been caused by something far more complex—anger with herself for having deluded herself for so long about Calvin, for having so naïvely believed herself to be in love with him.

For much of their acquaintance and all of their engagement, he had been totally selfish towards her. He had used her feelings for him as fuel with which to feed his pride. He had basked in what he had interpreted as adoration but which, she acknowledged at last, had been on her part mere hero-worship.

'Fought your battle?' Marsh asked mockingly. 'Who was the victor?'

Her face lifted in a brilliant smile. 'I, me, myself.'

'All three?' He pretended to frown. 'It was some fight! But, three against one,' he shook his head, smiling, 'your adversary didn't stand a chance. Feeling better now?'

'Fine, absolutely and deliciously fine.'

He laughed, head thrown back, and it was Calvin's turn to look round. He scowled and Shona, actuated still by the revenge motive, put her hand on Marsh's arm. Marsh glanced down at it, then at Calvin and finally at Shona. His lids lowered a fraction but he allowed the long-fingered, pink-nailed hand to remain.

A man approached, his smile broadening his already

rounded face. He was of medium height and his hair was greying slightly.

'Marsh! You look as though you're enjoying yourself.' His keen glance passed to Shona. 'Still finding the ladies irresistible?'

'You're letting me down, David,' Marsh commented goodhumouredly. 'I expected more gratitude from you, having saved you one more hand to shake—or maybe you didn't notice me escorting Miss Carroll into the room? I told the officer not to bother to call out my name.'

Shona recognised the man as the Captain and looked with awe upon the gold stripes signifying his high rank.

'I must,' said the Captain, 'have been too overwhelmed by the lady's charms to have noticed you.'

Marsh laughed again and as Shona felt him move, she realised with embarrassment that her hand still rested on his arm. She removed it quickly, but not before Captain Forth had noticed.

'I do believe,' said the Captain, 'I'm witnessing a miracle. Would Miss Carroll be Mr Marsh Faraday's "lady"?'

There was a breath of a pause before Marsh answered, his smile enigmatic. 'Indeed yes,' was the delayed reply. 'Marsh Faraday has found himself a lady to whom he can really refer as "his lady", at last.'

CHAPTER FIVE

THE concert had gone well. The audience had seemed extra appreciative. Calvin departed at once, leaving Shona to collect the music.

'I'm going for a drink with Toni,' he had said. In a moment Toni had appeared at his side and they had gone off together.

So that's the end of my evening, Shona thought, tidying the music scores into a pile. A white-haired lady who had spoken to her the first evening approached, looking genuinely concerned. 'I'm so glad you've made up your quarrel with that young man,' she said, 'that——' she pointed after Calvin, 'that flute player. I heard you arguing this morning and you did say some bitter words to each other.'

Shona coloured deeply. 'I'm sorry about that. The microphone had been left on by mistake and we didn't know. Anyway,' she managed a reassuring smile, 'it's a good thing we're friends again.' Shona thought bitterly, We're not even that. 'Otherwise,' she went on, 'there might have been a terrible jumble of sounds coming from our instruments this evening!'

The lady laughed. 'I do think you play beautifully,' she said.

'Oh, you mean Calvin. Yes, he's a really brilliant flautist. Everyone says he's got star quality and——'

The lady put her hand on Shona's arm. 'Well, to be honest, dear,' she whispered, 'I really meant you.'

'But I only accompany Calvin,' Shona protested.

'Never mind that,' said the lady, 'it comes through, your wonderful playing, even though you're trying to hold it back so that he can have the limelight.'

Again Shona coloured, looking around desperately in

search of some diversion which would halt the lady's embarrassing praise.

Her gaze came to a swerving stop at the barrier of two grey-green, watching eyes. She had not noticed Marsh leaning, hands in pockets, against the piano. At the sight of him, the thought that he had overheard the praise confused her so much that she began shuffling the pile of music scores as if they were a pack of cards.

'Dear me,' said the lady, following her eyes, 'I do hope I haven't upset the applecart, but I just had to tell you how good you were. I wish you would play more solo items. I mean, the flute playing is lovely, but—well, to be absolutely honest, I think you're better!'

She gave a little wave and disappeared into the crowds.

Marsh said, with a lazy smile, 'That paper will be in tatters if you don't stop fiddling with it.'

Shona's hands jerked from the music. She said, challengingly, 'I hope you enjoyed that little titbit of gossip you overheard.'

'So tart she is,' Marsh drawled, 'and after such praise, too.'

'I hope you now think I'm worth my keep.'

'That,' he remarked, his eyes moving over her shapeliness, 'will only be put to the test when I start "keeping" you, won't it?'

'You know very well what I'm referring to,' Shona flung back. 'The contract.'

'Were you?' he replied, with mock innocence. He dwelt for a moment on her wide mouth. 'Maybe now that you're Marsh Faraday's "lady", we should draw up another contract. Strictly between ourselves, of course.'

As she picked up the music and held it against her like a shield, she snapped, 'You're twisting my words and my meanings. You know what I really meant.'

He strolled towards her. 'Yes, I agree that it seems, in one passenger's eyes at least, that you're worth the money we're paying you. Not to mention your free passage.' He flicked a few strands of her hair in a familiar gesture.

He went on, 'With regard to the lady's comments, I always value the feedback we get from passengers, whether it's in the form of criticism or praise. It helps us plan our future cruises, particularly, as in this case, on the entertainments side.'

'Does that mean,' she smiled provocatively 'that now you've heard a verbal reference in my favour, you'll invite me back on board to entertain the passengers again?'

' "Me"?' he picked up her error at once. 'Surely it should have been "us"? It is, after all, a joint contract with your fiancé. You surely wouldn't consider leaving your future husband high and dry and come on a cruise as a piano soloist without him?'

She began to walk towards the swing doors. Marsh walked beside her. 'Let's get two things straight, Mr Faraday. One, I'm not my f——' she corrected herself to Marsh's amusement, 'Calvin's regular accompanist. And two,' they were through the swing doors, 'I'm not a soloist, either. I'm a teacher of the piano.'

'But haven't you played as a soloist with orchestras?'

Shona found the blue carpet on which they were standing suddenly fascinating. 'Now and then.' She looked up. 'But it's Calvin who's the star.'

'As you keep saying.' After a pause, he commented, 'I noticed that you assured the lady passenger that you'd made up your quarrel with your partner.'

She shrugged. 'Calvin and I often argue. Anyway,' she prepared to leave him, 'in the world of show business, it's well known that even couples who are about to announce their divorce often declare publicly their undying love for each other.'

'So,' Marsh persisted, 'like so many of them, you're living a lie, is that it?'

His clever questioning had brought her face to face with the truth, but nothing in the world would force her to admit it.

'How I live is my business,' she answered. 'My life's my

own. And I wish you'd keep out of it,' she threw over her shoulder as she walked away.

'Your wish will be granted, Miss Carroll,' he called after her curtly.

Shona walked restlessly about her cabin. Many times she passed her reflection in the long mirror, but she kept her head averted. She wandered to the window and pulled aside the curtains which the cabin steward had drawn.

The sea was by no means calm, but although the ship was rolling enough to make the curtains sway, it was a movement she could easily accept. As Marsh had promised, the weather was kinder now.

Resuming her wanderings, she paused this time to consider her reflection, then turned away impatiently. That was the self who had tolerated unprotestingly Calvin's casual treatment of her, in spite of the fact that she was his wife-to-be. That was the girl whose abilities he had constantly disparaged, thus diminishing her self-confidence and, worse, her talent in her own eyes.

So persuading was he that she lacked that touch of fire and inspiration which thrust gifted people to the top of their professions, she had accepted Calvin's own assessment that she was little more than an amateur despite her paper qualifications, and that the only possible way she could earn a reasonable living was to become a teacher of the piano.

She walked to the bed which had been made up by the steward and absentmindedly touched the filmy softness of her nightgown which had been spread across the pillow. Calvin's assessment was wrong, she told herself fiercely. She was more than just a gifted amateur. Hadn't that white-haired lady told her? That white-haired lady! She was an appreciative listener, no more, no less. Certainly she was no fellow-musician. She had liked the sounds she had heard, that was all.

Calvin was a musician like herself, which meant that Calvin knew what he was talking about. His musical judgment was more to be relied upon than that of a kindly passenger.

There was a knock at the door and Shona came to a stop in the middle of the cabin. Was it Calvin, summoned up by her thoughts of him? Putting a welcoming smile on her face, she opened the door. Outside was a cabin steward, and in his hands was a box, a white box tied with coloured ribbon. A note hung loosely from that ribbon.

'Miss Carroll?' the steward asked. Shona nodded. 'This is for you.'

'Oh, but—I'm not expecting anything,' Shona declared, trying to gather her wits.

The steward smiled. 'An admirer, madam?' he asked.

'Oh, but——' For goodness' sake, she thought, I must take the box and end this stupid conversation. The door closed and she was left holding the box.

The label, she noted, was in fact a small envelope with her name scrawled upon it. When she saw the writing, her heart began to thump. Placing the box on the stool, she proceeded to untie the ribbon, her hands shaking a little. She told herself again not to be so stupid. It must be from Calvin, she thought, who else——? The writing on the envelope was not Calvin's.

Before opening the box, she withdrew the card from the envelope. The note said, 'To the girl who left her money behind, From the man who took his with him.'

The lid opened and Shona's hand, still shaking, went inside to lift out the box's contents. It was the Spanish doll she had so regretfully left behind in the souvenir shop at Vigo! It was not the smaller doll, but the larger one, dressed resplendently in purple, her first choice which she had dismissed only because of its greater cost.

Her cheeks grew pink. How long had Marsh stood at that shop door? For most of the time she had been in the shop, it seemed. The doll stood on a semi-circular wire stand which was attached to its feet. These were in a position for dancing. The body of the doll was half turned, the arms raised, one to waist height, the other lifted from the shoulder.

The hair was a dense black, bearing a purple rose to one side. In the ears were pearl studs. The face was smiling and provocative. The dress was of a silky satin and the over-dress of white lace. There were two layers of this, hanging stiffly to cover the doll's feet. Draped gracefully from the turned head was a white lace mantilla.

When Shona put the doll down, she found that her eyes were moist. The doll she loved, it was just what she wanted, it would be a reminder of the cruise—but most of all it would remind her of the man who had, in such a thoughtful gesture, given it to her.

'Given' it? Was that what he had done? Or had she mis-read that card? Maybe it was not a gift. Had he bought it for her because, as the card had said, he had the money with him, whereas she had not? Did he expect her to re-pay him?

It was something she must know—and know at once. And even if it was a gift, could she accept it? She was en-gaged, so how could she accept a present from another man? The thought came, rocking her like the ship beneath her feet. Why not? Why shouldn't she accept another man's present?

Why—why shouldn't she use Marsh's gift to taunt Cal-vin, to make him jealous? She held the doll to her cheek. She did not consider whether her scheme to reclaim Calvin from Toni's clutches was just, nor whether she wanted a man who was so easily diverted from his fiancée by another woman's practised charms. It was, at that moment, a plan which filled her with a strange pleasure.

The empty box was pushed into a wardrobe, the note into a drawer. The doll she took into her hands. It was time she stopped thinking. She would go into action, and the most important action she had to take was to thank the man who had given her the doll. Without pausing to wonder whether he would be in his cabin at this comparatively early hour of the evening, she took the lift to the deck on which his suite was situated.

Other passengers joined her in the lift and praised the doll. They asked her where she had found it and she told them, Vigo. All the women wished they had bought one, too. When she got out, they waved as the lift doors closed.

It took a few minutes to locate the Seascape Suite. Crew members of different categories passed her, but she did not like to ask them. They would know the man who occupied it and would wonder why she was seeking him out. Then she recalled the number he had given the steward when he had asked for a quilt to be brought from his cabin to hers. Cabin W 61, he had directed. She turned the corner and the door was there in front of her.

Even as she lifted her hand to knock she realised that, early as it was, he might still be in one of the bars, chatting with his officer friends and acquaintances. Holding the Spanish dancing doll in front of her with both hands, she waited, eyes studying its colour, its lively posture, its grace.

She would try once more, she decided, and raised her hand—only to find the door swinging away from her. The occupant of the Seascape Suite was at home to visitors.

Not, it seemed, to *welcome* them, if the expression in his eyes was anything to go by. Or was it the particular visitor who now stood looking up at him with large limpid eyes, and a small smile curving her mouth? *I wish you'd keep out of my life*, were the last words she had said to him that evening. *Your wish will be granted*, had been his acid reply.

Now she was in the cabin, looking round, her breath stolen from her by the size, the elegance, the sheer indulgence of the luxury suite this man occupied. To her right and standing against the peacock blue of the pulled curtains was a long couch. To one side was a writing table and chair. In the centre was a coffee table, and armchairs at an angle to the table.

Across the cabin and against the opposite wall was a wood-encased refrigerator. Farther along was a built-in

radio and music system. Next to that was a telephone table
bearing a telephone. Eyes still staring, her head turned to
the left to encounter floor-to-ceiling drapes, caught back
in the open position. These, she assumed dazedly, would
for daytime use be pulled across to divide the sleeping
area from the sitting room.

Now they revealed the sleeping area which appeared,
from where Shona stood, to be even more spacious than
the living area. There was, beyond that, yet another door
leading, probably, to a bathroom. Two beds were separated
by a table on which were shaded lamps, ash trays and
magazines. Across the bedroom section was a dressing-
table, wardrobes and chests of drawers.

There were stools and chairs and the entire area from
one end of the cabin to the other was covered in wall-to-
wall gold-coloured carpeting. The bedcovers were in gold,
the diffused lighting shed a golden glow. That glow shone
in Shona's eyes as she turned in silence to her reluctant
host.

'Has the sight of so much luxury rendered you speech-
less?' he asked with heavy sarcasm. 'Or are you horrified
that, with so much poverty in the world, one man is occupying a suite which is clearly meant for two, but into which
could be fitted, at a pinch, half the population of a small
village?'

'Such thoughts hadn't even entered my head,' she returned. 'If you choose to feel guilty about having so much
money that you can afford to pay for all this, that's
your——' A thought flashed across her mind. 'You're not
travelling *free*?'

'Aren't you?'

It was tantamount to a confession that he was! 'That's
different. I mean, I'm not on my vacation, I'm working——'

'And getting paid for it, in addition to your free passage.'

For a moment the statement silenced her. Then she said,
'It's the old story, isn't it? I quote,' her eyes challenged
his, '*Unto every one that hath shall be given, and he shall
have abundance.*'

His eyes were like glinting ice as he turned, gripped her shoulders and pushed her backwards towards the door.

'Please, please,' she gasped, 'I'm sorry. I didn't intend to give offence, especially to you.'

'You're lying. You had every intention of giving insult, *especially to me*. "Keep out of my life," you said. I agreed wholeheartedly to do so. So why have you come walking in here?' His bruising hands released her and she rubbed a shoulder.

'I—I think it's wonderful, all of it. And—and I'm sure you deserve to be allocated such a beautiful cabin. After all, you are a director of the company, and——'

'Thanks,' he interrupted acidly, 'for those few kind words, but I'm paying a high price, a very high price, for this suite. I'm using it only because it would otherwise have gone the whole cruise without an occupant.'

Shona looked down at the doll, running a gentle finger over the delicate white lace mantilla. 'Sorry again.'

He strolled across to the refrigerator, opening it and taking out two bottles. 'A drink?' She nodded. 'Name your poison.' She told him, 'Sherry, please.' He reached up and took two glasses from a cabinet. 'Please sit down,' he invited and Shona sank on to the couch. As he poured, he asked, 'Why did you come?'

Shona looked around then Marsh was standing in front of her, a glass in each hand. He looked at her holding the doll as if it were a treasure beyond price.

'This doll,' she said, and stopped. It was no good, she had to finish the sentence simply because she had to know the answer. 'I'd like to know how much I owe you.'

'So you came to insult me again? Let me show you the door, Miss Carroll.' Some of the ice in his eyes had broken away and filtered into his voice. He bent to put down the drinks, but Shona's hand shot out intercepting the movement and taking the glass.

He watched her, narrow-eyed. 'You'll find it difficult walking the decks of a slightly rolling ship with an almost full glass in your hand.'

Her smile was small but determined. 'I intend, Mr Faraday, to sit right here and drink it.'

'So you're forcing me to play the reluctant host?'

She raised the glass to her lips to drink in some courage to resist whatever action he might take to eject her.

'I shouldn't, if I were you.'

Her look was questioning, moving from the glass to his face. 'Is it really "poison", as you called it? Don't you want my dead body on your hands?'

'I'd rather have your live body on my hands.'

The comment made her cheeks glow.

'I think that's my kind of drink,' his hand came out and took the glass, 'unless the taste of the hard stuff makes you feel like a real sailor, instead of just a passenger on a cruise?' He handed her the other glass and watched a third of it being swallowed at a gulp.

'I didn't mean to insult you,' she told him, dabbing at her lips with a handkerchief. 'I just didn't want to be in the wrong by looking on something as a gift, when it was really meant as a kindly gesture. After all, your note was quite correct. I did leave my money behind, and you did have yours with you. What you did—buying it for me, that is—could have been intended as a loan.'

'It was intended as a gift.'

In the face of his stiff manner, she reacted stiffly, too. 'Thank you very much. It was very kind of you.' How to convey to him her pleasure in possessing the dancing doll, in the fact that it was a present from him, something to keep and gaze at, remembering the cruise, remembering him . . .

'Something to remember me by.' It was as though he had read her thoughts, but his eyes mocked. He sat beside her and lifted his drink, savouring its taste. 'How will you explain it away to your fiancé? Lie to him and say you bought it yourself?'

'Why should I pretend? I'll tell him you gave it to me.'

'Use it as a way to make him jealous, to bring him to heel again?' He put down his empty glass and reached out, taking the doll. 'Will he do this, do you think?' His hands closed round the doll, one grasping the body, the other the skirt. Then he twisted the doll as if it were a wet rag.

Shona gasped, covering her mouth with a shaking hand, gazing in horror at the result of his action. She felt as if he were squeezing her and her very life-blood was staining his hands ...

'Stop it!' she shrieked. 'You've ruined it. Give it to me! You're nothing but a brute, a vandal.' Tears invaded her voice. 'It was beautiful, I loved it, I've never wanted anything more than I wanted to keep that doll.'

The doll was still in his destructive grip and Shona sprang at him, clawing at his hands, pulling at his arms, then, as he still would not let go, hitting him wherever she could reach.

He laughed, which enraged her even more. Suddenly the doll was free. It was there on her knees, standing with its skirts still swirling, its arms upraised, its mantilla as perfectly arranged as if no hand had ever touched it. Shona's gasp this time was of astonishment and relief. 'How——?' she choked.

'The woman in the shop demonstrated its near-indestructibility to me, intending I think to show how easily the doll could be packed in a suitcase.'

Accusing eyes turned to his. 'And you did it to torment me!'

'Are you going to hit me again?' he asked conversationally.

'I'd like to. I'd like to—to——' She dared not tell him what in her heart she wanted to do.

'Would you?' It seemed he had already guessed. She found herself in his arms, felt his lips on hers, lifting, stroking, tantalising in their lightness of touch. Her arms crept—of their own accord, she told herself frantically—around his neck and she discovered, with a shock, that her mouth was straining, straining to catch at his, to keep his kisses for fear that they might be lost to her for ever.

Foolish thoughts chased each other through her mind,

and then she wasn't thinking at all, only feeling—her breasts crushed against his chest, his thighs pressing hers, his hands caressing the feminine shape of her ... His touch, incredibly, warm against the softness of her flesh. By then she had gone too far into the forest of his lovemaking to care about how his hands had strayed so far from the accepted pathways.

When his mouth left hers and his hold lightened, she rested, exhausted, against him, the feel of his chest beneath his opened shirt a hard haven against her cheek.

'Shona.' His voice was husky, his lips warm on her forehead.

'You've done to me what you did to the doll,' she whispered. 'Grasped me and twisted me and crushed me. Then you let me go and here I am, back to being what I always was.' Not quite, she thought, because that kiss will always stay with me, never leaving me even though one day soon he'll walk away.

'So now you like the touch of my lips, instead of hating them as you told me the last time?'

'I'm an engaged woman,' she prevaricated, looking up at him with mischief in her eyes.

'You don't say?' he drawled. 'Engaged to whom? To the brilliant flute player who's fooling around at the moment with another woman instead of enjoying himself with his bride-to-be? Or are you engaged to the shipping company director, who's been on the brink of marriage himself twice, but has managed each time to evade the noose his fiancées have thrown at his head?'

Shona pulled herself upright, disentangling her arms, as anger brought sparks to her eyes. 'You're despicable,' she hissed. 'You're mean, you think you're heaven's gift to women——'

She was swung across him, dragged on to his lap and her abuse was stilled by the ruthless hardness of his mouth. Against her will, her body began to melt, to respond, to cling and give back the kisses she received. When her flesh began to tingle as probing fingers found their way back to the cleft between her breasts, reason began to prevail over instinct and reason won the battle.

'No,' she muttered, unable to speak more clearly because of the pressure of his mouth, 'no and again no.'

'My sweet,' he said softly, 'it's yes and yes again. All the signs are there, the shy, provocative signals. *Take me, I'm yours.* That's what you're saying.'

Anger gave her struggles to free herself greater impetus, but if he had not let her go—suddenly, just as he had released the doll—she would have been powerless against his greater strength. Moments later she was beside him, smoothing her skirt—until she saw that some of the tiny buttons at the front of her dress had broken free of their buttonholes. So that was how he had trespassed!

She glared at him. 'You had no right, no right at all.'

'None whatsoever,' he agreed, 'but didn't you enjoy the fact that I did!'

Indignantly she rose to go, but Marsh pulled her back beside him. 'There's something I must know. How often does Calvin Faber make love to you?' She started again to pull away, but he said, 'You have every right to tell me to mind my own business.'

It was a trick, and a clever one, but she told him the truth all the same. 'He kisses me—now and then. We walk together and talk together and—and play together.' With a quick smile, 'The flute and the piano, I mean.' She frowned. 'But never like you——' she picked up the doll which had fallen to the floor, 'like the way you——' She had to stop, because this was a cynical man, one who had, in his own words, escaped the 'noose' twice. A man who, she had said to his face and he had not refuted her statement, would make love to a woman not because he liked her, but because he liked making love.

He rested against the couch back, eyes closed as if deep in thought. Then he said, patting the cushion which now separated them, 'Come here.'

Since she had not completely extricated herself from his magnetic aura and was, therefore, still under his spell, she obeyed, clutching the Spanish doll.

'Tell me,' he took her hand, removing the doll and putting it on a table, 'do you want your fiancé to make love to you?'

There was a tiny pause, unexplained even to herself. 'Are you going to suggest,' she asked, her brown eyes touched with doubt, 'what I think you are?'

'To act in such a way as to make your fiancé jealous— yes, that was in my mind. A collaboration between the two of us, a makebelieve love affair to help you and——' he looked at her, 'it would help me, too.' He did not explain how it would help him. 'It's an ancient remedy and often a potent one. Agreed?'

Shona frowned, trying to imagine Calvin being jealous of any other man who might appear to attach himself to her. A picture formed of Toni reaching out and taking Calvin's hand and of Calvin going willingly without a backward glance. It aroused within her a longing to prove to him that *someone* found her attractive—even if it was pretence from start to finish, as she knew it would be. And —her heart gave a lamb-like leap—that 'someone' would be Marsh Faraday. Which, she thought, hugging herself in the region of her heart, was perhaps the most important part of the whole thing ...

Looking up at him brightly, Shona answered, 'It's worth a try. But,' her doubts returned, 'you'd have to be a very good actor.' She did not mention that, in playing such a part, she wouldn't be acting at all. 'And there's another thing. Your status. Everyone knows who you are.'

'Which means, my sweet girl, that I hold all the cards, including the ace.' With a spark in his eyes, he added, 'And that's a card I'll play at exactly the right time.'

The statement puzzled her. Then her brow cleared and she smiled. 'I suppose you mean producing an engagement ring, although I know, and you know, that to you that wouldn't mean a thing, because you're in the habit of breaking engagements which is something you've done twice before. Your mother said so.'

'My mother says a darned sight too much at times. Come here, woman,' impatiently he pulled her towards him, 'let's start as we mean to go on.' She did not attempt to resist for one simple reason—she did not want to. As his mouth descended, slowly, slowly, and her anticipation of her pleasure at the touch of it grew, her conscience stirred, like a lion cub uncurling, stretching—and returning to sleep.

He commented, his lips flicking hers, 'Did I remember to tell you how much I like your eyes, your face, your hair, your shape? But more than anything at this moment, I like the look of your mouth. And,' huskily, 'how much I want to taste it.'

'Marsh,' it was a token protestation, 'I must go. There's no need, now.' His eyes looked deep into hers. 'There's no one to see.'

'Which is all the better,' he commented, smiling faintly —was it with mockery? 'It means we can practise our make-believe love in complete privacy.'

There was, she thought dreamily, no answer to that, no answer at all.

CHAPTER SIX

SHONA did not knock at Calvin's door, thus forcing him to accompany her to breakfast. She had, she told herself, too much pride. But as she neared the lower deck on which the restaurant was situated, she had second and third thoughts. Suppose he was still waiting patiently for her in his cabin?

He was seated, behind his menu, at the table. Verity Faraday was there, too, but there was no sign of her son. Disappointed, Shona forgot to say 'good morning' until Mrs Faraday welcomed her with the word. Startled, Shona responded in kind, emerging from her memory of Marsh's goodnight kiss outside her cabin door. Just in case Calvin comes along, Marsh had said. Calvin had not come along, and Shona would not have cared if he had.

Now she said loudly, 'Good morning, Calvin.'

He lifted the menu, looked her over indifferently and said, 'Hi.'

Toni's language, Shona noted. How long had he spent in her cabin last night? Then she remembered her pact with Marsh. A tingle of remembered pleasure brought a smile to her face as she thought, glancing at the face she had once admired above all other men's, I have a weapon to fight *you* with now.

'Marsh, darling!' Verity Faraday greeted her son as he pulled out his chair and sat down. 'It's unusual for you to be last.'

He glanced around the table, nodding to an unresponsive Calvin and to the girl who was seated on his right. 'There has to be a first time,' he answered his mother, 'for everything. Even being last.'

'Did you drink and dance into the small hours,' his mother asked, 'and wake up with a hangover?'

'An inspired guess, Mother,' he answered, looking at no one, 'but wrong. However,' he affected a satisfied sigh, 'I did entertain—someone.'

'So you had an entertaining evening, after all,' his mother persisted.

'Very.'

'Did you—er—make progress?' There was a knowing twinkle in his mother's eye.

'Er——' he smiled faintly as he picked up the menu, 'let's just say——' he paused, 'I'm working on it.'

During this family exchange, Shona had read the breakfast menu from beginning to end and back to the beginning, yet she could not remember a word. 'Entertainment' ... 'progress' ... 'working on it'. What was Marsh Faraday playing at? Had he forgotten their agreement already?

'Remember, Marsh,' Verity smiled at the eyes and forehead of her son, which was all she could see above his menu card, 'that your days are numbered. Every cruise, whether long or short, has a beginning and an end.'

'Mm,' her son put his menu down, having apparently decided on his choice, 'a few days—too little time.' It was as if he was speaking to himself.

The waiter came and when he had gone with the orders Calvin said, bringing his roving eyes back to home ground —having sought, Shona knew, for a sight of Toni Hardy, 'There isn't going to be an evening concert tonight.' With a quick defensive glance at Marsh Faraday, he added, 'It's in accordance with the contract.'

'So we can relax today?' Shona queried.

'I suppose so. But when breakfast's over I'd like to discuss tomorrow evening's programme with you.'

Shona sipped the orange juice which had been placed in front of her. She said tentatively, 'One or two people have asked me if I'd play more solo pieces.'

Calvin tackled his grapefruit cocktail, eating the cherry first. 'Why?' His voice was belligerent, the question revealing the inflated size of his professional ego. Although Shona was more than familiar with Calvin's vanity, it still shocked her to hear it so blatantly expressed.

Their companions, eating their melon, could not have overlooked the revelation of this side of Calvin's nature. Mrs Faraday appeared slightly shocked, while her son continued—had he suddenly turned deaf?—with his breakfast.

Shona shrugged, a little helpless in the face of such conceit. 'I think they must like my playing.'

'Look,' said Calvin, 'you came on this cruise as my accompanist, not as a concert pianist.'

Shona was silent. The next course was delivered to their table with a flourish. Talking was suspended for a while. At length Verity asked, 'What are your plans for this morning, Marsh?'

'If the weather keeps its promise of the early morning, I'll be at one of the swimming pools.'

'Do you get up early every day?' It was the first time Shona had addressed Marsh since he had appeared.

'When—er——' a smile gave a tinge of colour to his flicking glance, 'I sleep alone.'

'Didn't I tell you about my son and women, Shona!' Verity exclaimed.

Shona's eyes swung to meet Marsh's taunting gaze. 'You did. He warned me himself, too.' If he could play with her, then she would return the compliment. 'About being clever and freeing himself of two engagements. In my opinion, it's even more clever to catch *and keep* a woman. *And far less cowardly!*'

Marsh's fingers pushed his empty cup away. His mouth hardened, his eyes narrowed. 'When your opinion is wanted, it'll be asked for.' He rose. 'Please excuse me. See you around, Mother.' He walked out of the restaurant.

It took Calvin about an hour to discuss with Shona the music they would play at the following evening's concert. By the way he kept looking at his watch, it was obvious that he wished the hour could have been cut by half.

'Do we practise today?' Shona asked.

Calvin glanced out of his cabin window and Shona followed his eyes. She saw the waves dancing in the sunlight, felt the benign movement of the ship as it glided through the water. 'No,' Calvin told her. 'Like our high and mighty shipping company director, I'll be swimming too.'

'That's a good idea,' Shona commented, more to discover Calvin's reaction than to let him know she might be following his example.

'I've arranged to meet Toni,' said Calvin, rubbing a cloth over the shining metal of his flute.

'Good,' she retorted from the door, 'because I'm going to look for Danny and maybe discuss an idea we had.'

'What idea?' Calvin called after her.

Her answer was a self-satisfied smile just before she closed the door. Let him wonder, she laughed inwardly. Although in her heart she doubted if he gave the matter another thought.

Shona stepped through the double swing doors on to the open deck. Beyond the rail the sea swell stretched into the seemingly limitless distance. Her eyes scanned the horizon, seeing dots which, through binoculars, would almost certainly materialise into the shape of other ships, tankers, maybe even a cruiser like the *Sea Wanderer*.

Her eyes moved nearer home. Her head turned first right, then left. This time she sought for the shape of a man whose outline she would recognise on sight. She needed air, she told herself, she would give herself the task of walking round the decks until—until her lungs were full. Even to herself she would not admit the truth.

It was almost coffee time before she found him. He was sea-gazing, like so many other passengers she had come across on her walk, staring at the space, the distance, as if they had difficulty in taking in just how small the land masses of the earth were in relation to the size of the oceans. It was as if they refused to believe they were personally of such relative insignificance that their existence or non-existence did not greatly matter in the history of the universe.

When Shona walked silently to Marsh's side, it did not

seem that such profound thoughts were the cause of his totally serious expression. It was more as though he was submerged in problems of a more personal nature—business, commerce, the world of finance. He of all people, Shona told herself, would entertain no doubts or uncertainties as to his relative importance in the world's affairs.

For a few seconds she stood behind and to the left of him. The wind lifted her hair, billowed her shirt-blouse, flapped at her slacks. The sun was turning on its heat, promising a golden day.

'Marsh?' Her voice was small against the swish of the wash, the persistent throb of the engines. She moved to his side.

'Yes?' He had not looked round, keeping his expression to himself. The indifference in his tone was almost a rebuff. Had the kisses and the loving and the promises of last night really happened or had they all been part of her night's dreaming?

'I'm sorry about what I said at breakfast.' There was no reaction. 'It was just that—well, you seemed to have forgotten last night. The arrangement we made.' He stared at the restless sea. 'Our—our agreement.' His silence was making her hesitant.

He spoke at last, keeping his head averted. 'What did you expect me to do? Throw my arms round your neck, stage a love scene in public? Under Calvin Faber's nose? Not to mention hundreds of half-awake passengers.'

'No, of course not, but——'

'But what?' He turned, resting an elbow on the topmost rail, leaning on his thigh. 'You're an engaged woman. Solve your own problems. If your husband-to-be shows signs of straying, ask yourself why.' His eyes meandered over her, noting the neat waist, the shapely hips, the slender legs outlined by the breeze beneath the fabric of the slacks. 'Maybe if you kissed him like you kissed me last night, he wouldn't have looked elsewhere for his fun.'

Her cheeks flushed as if she had suddenly developed sunburn. 'Will you stop insulting me!' She gripped the rail, staring out to sea. Passengers passed to and fro behind them. 'So you want to go back on your promise to help me.'

He was inspecting her profile and she knew it. 'Did I make a promise, Shona?' He turned to lean forward on his elbows, gazing as she was into the distance.

Her bottom lip, which she had compressed to control it, fought free and trembled slightly. 'A collaboration, you called it,' she said 'A—a makebelieve love affair, to help me and——' She remembered that he had not completed the sentence. 'And I said you'd—we'd have to be very good actors.'

He turned a dazzling smile upon her and it was as though she had tipped a glass of burning spirits down her throat. 'Maybe it was the acting part that's got me worried.' The heady sensation began to pass.

'You mean you couldn't even begin to pretend that you were attracted to me?'

Slowly he straightened, took her by the shoulders and turned her to face him. He looked her over from head to foot, his gaze lingering at last on the shape beneath the shirt, the white throat that rose from the low-buttoned neckline, the rounded chin, the brown anxious eyes.

His hands fell away to push into the pockets of his tight-fitting sand-coloured pants. His back was to the sun which cast his features into shadow. 'It would be difficult, one of the most difficult things I've ever done.'

'You must be joking,' she choked.

Marsh faced the sea again. 'Unfortunately, no.' His voice, like his face, was serious.

The ship's clock nearby clicked noisily to the half-hour. He took her hand. 'Okay, so in the madness of midnight we made a bargain. I'll do my best to keep that bargain. But when I said it wouldn't be easy, I meant it.'

Shona attempted to tug her hand from his. 'Forget we ever made it. It's plain I'm just not your type, so there's no need to insult me. I can take a hint.'

'You're not my usual type, my sweet. But I'd be a fool to refuse the chance of having a girl as attractive as you in my arms, however devious the reason. So let's have coffee together. We've got to start somewhere.'

It was as they were walking to the coffee lounge, with Marsh's arm flung carelessly across her shoulders, that Shona realised just what she had let herself in for. Every member of the crew they passed, from the lowest to the highest, appeared to know who Marsh was. Doors were opened, salutes acknowledged with brief nods. The coffee waiter materialised at their table as if a gun had been fired.

Marsh leaned back, legs crossed, as they drank their coffee. Shona leaned forward. One or two people she recognised from the concert audiences waved to her, looking with curiosity at her companion.

Marsh said, looking beyond her, then at her, his eyes half open, 'Did you say earlier you intended looking for Danny Mercer? Seems he's looking for you, too.'

As Shona's head turned Marsh sat forward, putting down his coffee cup. Danny was gazing round, then spotted her, lifting a hand and making for them.

'Hi,' said Danny, coming to a stop. 'Heard you wanted me.' He grinned. 'And boy, do I want you!'

Marsh removed himself from his chair, saying to Shona, 'See you around, maybe.'

His voice was so dry she felt impelled to call, 'Marsh?' He wasn't even out of earshot, yet he didn't respond.

Danny took the empty chair, pushing his long fair hair from his eyes. The shadows beneath them told of late nights, yet the look in them spoke of a half-hidden vulnerability. Shona needed no telling that he would have preferred Toni to be sitting where she herself sat.

'This musical thing I suggested. Are you game to try?'

'Ready for anything musically, Danny,' Shona assured him, smiling.

'Okay, then, let's find a cosy corner with a piano. The theatre's probably empty at this time.'

Shona seated herself at the piano, Danny leaned against it on his elbows. 'Who'll start?' he asked. 'You? Me on my guitar? You? Okay.' He moved away, picked up his instrument and said, 'You do your thing while I do mine. I won't make a sound.'

'Are our musical memories compatible?' Shona asked.

'Don't worry,' Danny assured her, 'I'll remember every note.'

Shona nodded, then sat, head bowed, hands clasped on her lap, appreciating Danny's silence. All around there were sea-going sounds, the engine-throb which with its vibrations had the entire ship in its grip, the distant echoes of up-raised voices. From open windows came the sharp and constant patter of footsteps on deck. Shona's fingers hovered, stroked the keys and, as her brain dictated, began to play.

After a while Danny slipped, with professional ease, into the musical sound Shona was creating. Her fingers ran to the high notes and back to the lower, and the music was waves. Danny plucked at the strings, and there was the wind, a breeze at first, but as the piano notes grew louder and more menacing, from Danny's guitar there came a gale. Together they created a storm—of mind? Of the elements? Shona did not know. She was aware only of putting her very soul into her playing, but unaware of bringing Danny's performance with her to its heights.

As the storm died away, there was left only the punctuating throb of the ship's engines and the melting into a heart-rending melody of end-of-cruise partings and treasured memories evocative enough to bring sadness in the wake of remembered joy.

Shona slumped, drained of emotion. Danny stared at her bent head. 'Wow, kid!' he exclaimed. 'Are you great!'

Her head lifted and she smiled. 'Thanks, Danny, but I don't know where it came from. I can only say thanks to the part of myself that produced it. Honestly, it wasn't me!' They laughed together. 'Anyway, Danny, you were great yourself. Why are you wasting your talent doing the stuff you're being paid for here, when you could be a cult figure on the classical guitar scene?'

'Hey, you're a flatterer,' Danny laughed, going red. 'What do you want, Miss Carroll?' She made as if to lunge at him and he pretended to cower. 'Okay, I'm sorry, but deep down I'm a modest guy and—well,' he spread his hand over his face in an attitude of mock coyness, 'no girl's ever talked to me like that before. But seriously, you're a professional. Did you mean that?'

'I never say anything I don't mean, Danny.'

'I'll bear it in mind when the next two cruises are over. Okay? But it means going right back to the drawing board. It takes some guts to do that.'

'You're young enough, Danny.'

He plucked a string or two on his guitar. 'But you're a genius, really you are.'

Shona shook her head. 'Compared with Calvin, I'm a nothing, not even mediocre.'

'Quit fooling yourself. You're great, and I do mean great. Now, can we repeat that, then I'll see what I can do for a performance of our very own work this evening.'

'*Sea Wanderer* Concerto,' Shona suggested, 'for piano and guitar. Right?'

Danny nodded and they began again.

Shona found Verity at the lunch table. Calvin's seat was occupied by Verity's escort, John Victor. At Shona's bewildered look, Verity explained,

'Calvin called out that he was lunching with Toni. He's somewhere down there, I believe.' She indicated the large sunken area of the restaurant. 'He said would I explain.'

John Victor laughed rather heartily. 'He didn't explain what it was we should explain.'

'That's all right,' said Shona, but a shadow flitted across her features which Marsh, who had arrived as his mother had spoken, seemed to interpret as dismay at her fiancé's thoughtless treatment. It was really pique at his callous disregard of her feelings.

'I told you,' said Marsh, spreading his napkin, 'Toni's notorious on board for her casual affairs.'

'Really?' Shona turned on a flippant manner. 'Isn't there a clause in her contract which forbids her playing about with the passengers' finer feelings? Or don't the *Sea Wanderer*'s customers possess any finer feelings?'

'We'll let that pass,' Marsh replied curtly. He switched his attention in a manner calculated to imply contempt. 'Been sunbathing, Mother?'

The rest of the conversation followed a similar line until Mrs Faraday asked, 'And what has our sweet classical pianist been doing with herself this morning?'

'Entertaining another man,' Shona answered promptly, giving Marsh a provocative look.

'To your mutual enjoyment and satisfaction, no doubt?' Marsh commented cynically.

'No doubt at all.' Shona smiled challengingly. 'We—er——' she frowned and tapped her chin as if remembering, 'improvised and—er—invented and tried out new—er—themes.' She quirked an eyebrow at him and grinned.

'Did you now?' He looked her over assessingly. 'Maybe that wide-eyed air of purity you carry around with you is just a blind, and I've been taken in. You're a more worldly little package of femininity than I realised. I must remember that on——' he directed his gaze at the menu, 'certain appropriate occasions.'

'Behave, my son,' Verity reproved him with a smile. 'The prey isn't yours to pounce on.'

'When it's juicy and desirable and casts scent trails behind it,' was Marsh's drawled reply, 'then it can't complain if the predator springs and captures it and proceeds to tear it apart.' He looked meaningfully at Shona who immediately hid behind her menu. 'Besides, Mother, we're involved in a devious and very complicated game. Are we not, Shona, my love?'

'This,' said Verity to John Victor, 'is where I bow out of my son's private affairs. But how he's managed to get such a sweet young woman as this girl here caught up in his love life, I just don't know.'

'Don't worry, Mrs Faraday,' Shona said to the appetisers, soups, farinaceous and main courses, 'I'm not his type. He told me. Like Calvin I believe he goes for blondes.'

Verity frowned, then smiled. 'I doubt if the colour of their hair worries him much. But it's true that his two ex-fiancées were fair-haired.'

'There you are then,' said Shona, her stormy eyes meeting Marsh's amused glance, 'I'm quite safe from his clutches.'

'Is that a challenge?' Marsh drawled.

Instead of replying, Shona busied herself with her meal.

In her cabin after lunch, Shona seized the Spanish doll and gazed at it.

'If only you and I were blondes,' she said to the attractive face with its enticing eyes, 'we'd have that man Marsh Faraday at our feet. Then you could dance all over him, and I could walk all over him.' With a sigh she replaced the doll on the table.

It took ten minutes to change into her two-piece floral-patterned swimsuit and comb her silky hair. Slipping her feet into sandals and pulling on a towelling wrap, she tucked a rolled-up towel under her arm and pushed on sunglasses. After taking the lift, she walked through the blue-carpeted Pool Bar by which passengers passed to gain access to the swimming pool area.

With her eyes narrowed against the sun, she scanned the tiered decks which, at first, were a blur of colour, movement and faces. Then she saw Calvin in swimming trunks, re-clining in a deck chair. Beside him was Toni in a scarlet one-piece swimsuit, covering her arms and legs with sun-tan oil.

There was no sign of Marsh. Calvin's hand was raised, beckoning to Shona to join him. She had little choice but to make her way between glistening, half-clothed bodies and join him.

Toni said, 'Hi,' and Calvin asked, 'All alone?' His grin implied that though she might be on her own, he certainly was not.

Shona indicated the crowds. 'Hardly,' she countered, refusing to allow Calvin to win the point. The blue-tinted pool was an invitation she could not resist. Refusing Calvin's offer to find her a seat, she dropped her towel and sunglasses beside him and peeled off her robe.

She stood, arms raised to lift her hair, consciously posing to catch her fiancé's eye. And catch it she did. Glorying for a few seconds in revealing to him and to anyone else who was interested the attractions of her shapliness, she adjusted the straps of the bra top and smoothed her hands over her barely-covered hips. Her greatest pleasure, just before she walked to the pool's edge, was the sight of Toni staring, open-mouthed, at the girl whom she had plainly dismissed as of nil interest to any man.

'Shona!' Her fiancé was calling. Shona paused without turning.

'Leave her, Cal.'

'Shona!' Calvin had ignored his new-but-temporary girl-friend's coaxing. 'About tonight—what's this rumour I've heard about you and Danny——?'

Shona decided, in her turn, to ignore her fiancé's attempt to get her back to his side. Delighting, for the first time ever, in displaying all that nature had seen fit to bestow on her in the way of female attractions, she raised her arms again with the intention of diving into the half-occupied pool.

There was a blow in the small of her back. As she lurched forward, she shrieked, 'For heaven's sake, Calvin——!' and hit the water, winded and unprepared. There was a great splash beside her just before she went under. Seconds later she surfaced, gasping and furious. Wiping the water from her eyes, she choked.

'You bird-brained, idiot-minded fool, Calvin, I could have——' With her fingers outspread over her cheeks she saw Marsh Faraday running wet fingers through dripping hair. He was grinning and she knew that she had unfairly blamed Calvin.

Marsh was treading water beside her now and she lashed out with tongue and hands. 'Why, you rotten, miserable——' Her blows were landing ineffectively on his chest, his arms, anywhere that her water-heavy hands could reach.

With consummate ease he caught her wrists, bunching them into one hand and pulling her forward, face down, while with his other hand he aimed hard slaps on her rear.

'Stop it!' she screamed. 'Stop it, you louse!'

The blows grew harder and she kicked and twisted with all her might. He was hurting her so much the tears sprang and mixed with the pool water. People around were laughing, then when the rain of blows stopped, they turned away and carried on swimming.

Marsh dragged her still struggling body into a corner, releasing her wrists and gripping her shoulders until she was upright. 'Why?' she gasped on a sob, 'why?'

His eyes were as gleaming as the water running down him. 'Why? Because of the way you were displaying yourself up there, because of your provocation of your fiancé in public which should have been confined to the bedroom. And because I know, from what you said earlier, that you're a damned sight more knowledgeable about sensual matters than you've so far pretended to be. And finally because,' he pulled her the length of him so that she could feel everything about him, 'you also know what follows what I did to you. This.'

His mouth closed over hers and his hands beneath the water made themselves totally familiar with every line and curve of her, slipping under the bra top and caressing her full and piquant shape. Her arms lifted and, in a reflex action of pure delight, closed around his neck. She was limp against him and had no strength to refuse his hands permission to seek and find any part of her body they chose.

As the screaming and shouting around them faded in, so she realised how public was his lovemaking—because that was what it had amounted to.

'Marsh,' her arms still clung, her head dropped to rest against the water-streaked hair on his chest, 'this is wrong. All these people—what will they think?'

'That you're my woman. Which is exactly what you

wanted, wasn't it?' His voice was harsh, not soft as it should have been when a man had made himself as familiar with her body's curves and inlets, her hips and her thighs, as he had.

She drew away, holding on to the bar. 'Not everyone, Marsh. Only Calvin. That was the whole point of our—our arrangement.'

'When a woman uses a man to get back at the man she loves as you're using me, then she can't object to whatever comes her way from that man in the form of——' his eyes lingered where only a few minutes before his hands had so possessively been, 'intimacies,' he finished. 'In any case, judging by the way you were talking at lunchtime, you have an impudence to take me to task for treating you as I did, when you know all about *inventions, improvisations, themes*——'

'But, Marsh,' she said, aghast, treading water as he spread his arms along the bar, 'I didn't really mean what you think. Danny and I were——'

A dangerous light came into his eyes. 'You've said enough about Danny Mercer and you. From now on, my winsome-yet-wicked love partner, it'll be Marsh and I,' his arms swooped and caught her to him again, 'Marsh and I, or, as the case may be, Marsh and me. Get it? That is, until the end of the cruise brings about a parting of the ways. Until then, my water nymph, I'll give you something to remember me by. *And* reclaim your straying husband-to-be for you. For which charitable action I think I deserve more than a kiss or two, don't you?'

'You think that if you demand payment in any other way, I'd *lower* myself to give it?'

He flung back his head, laughing at her. 'Lower yourself, Miss Carroll, is right. On to the bed, the floor ... I'm not fussy.'

Her fists lifted and lunged. His reaction was lightning-quick and he leapt sideways, swimming from her arm over arm. Shona, still furious, pursued, but as he turned, knowing she was there, and made as if to catch her, she slithered away and went for the steps out of the pool.

As she ran, dripping, to her towel and robe, wrapping both about her, Calvin demanded, 'What the hell was going on between you and Faraday in that pool?'

'Mind your own business,' she snapped, and rubbed herself all over.

'My, some of us are high-flyers, aren't we?' commented Toni, examining her fast-tanning arms. 'One of the shipping company's directors. You can't get much higher than that on this ship, can you, unless it's the Captain, and he's middle-aged and married.'

'You mind your own business, too!' Shona snapped at her, much to her own surprise. Then she looked round, saw the changing cubicles and made for their comparative solitude.

Someone walked beside her. 'Angry, are we?' the deep voice questioned. 'Anger often arises from frustration which, after our very close relationship in the pool, is hardly surprising. So come into my parlour, said the shipping company director to the ship's tame pianist, and I'll finish the job. I think, after what you gave me under water, you deserve complete satisfaction on dry land. Don't you agree?'

He urged her towards the ship's interior, but she jerked away and dived into an empty cubicle, locking the door on him.

At dinner that evening it was Marsh who was missing. Verity Faraday smiled her irresistible smile and even had Shona, her emotions in an impossible turmoil, responding.

In Marsh's chair was John Victor, his dark hair having almost succumbed to the encroachment of the grey, his round face still reflecting a boyishness at heart. His relationship with Verity did seem not to have deepened into anything more than the friendship with which it began.

Shona, however, was not concerned with such matters. All she noticed was Marsh's absence. At her puzzled look, Verity explained,

'Marsh decided to join the Captain again. He thought you might have some technicalities to discuss with your fiancé.' Shona's frown persisted. Verity enlarged, 'Such as the music you're playing this evening.'

Shona shook her head. 'I'm performing with Danny, not Calvin——'

'Yes, what is this I keep hearing?' Calvin appeared and pulled out his chair. 'There's something on the notice board about a concerto written especially for this cruise. It doesn't say why and it doesn't say who by.'

Shona smiled, uncurling her table napkin. 'Wait and see, Calvin.'

'Don't you mean wait and hear?' he asked sulkily.

For the rest of the meal he scarcely spoke. The resulting three-sided conversation was conducted by Verity with tact and subtlety. At times, Shona's eyes strayed to the centre of the restaurant, catching only fleeting glimpses of Marsh as the people in between moved in conversation. When she asked herself why, after their shattering encounter in the pool that afternoon, she could hardly keep her eyes off him, she found an answer which was so alarming she could not confess it even to herself.

Among the gathering audience in the Orchid Room Shona saw a number of her faithful followers from the classical concerts. Since it had been made clear that Calvin was not playing that evening, she was surprised.

As she made her way to the small platform and the piano, lifting the billowing skirt of her ankle-length gown, she saw seated to one side Calvin and Toni. Near to them Verity sat with John Victor, and Shona lifted her hand at Verity's wave of encouragement. Of Marsh there was no sign. The excitement that was building up inside Shona's mind and body wavered and dulled a little. If he were there, she would perform just that little better, if only to show him—well, she thought, just to *show* him ...

Danny joined her, smiling and excited. She could see his eyes catching the coloured lights which illuminated the large room. 'I thought we'd start with some familiar tunes,' Danny said, 'and leave the concerto to the last.' He glanced round quickly. 'A bit of nostalgia would go down well, I think, don't you? That is, if you're game.'

'Old favourites, like——' Shona paused, then smiled, 'excerpts from *The Desert Song, New Moon*?' Danny nodded vigorously. 'But you'd have to sing them, Danny.'

'So what? I'm not a musical moron. I know the words. Romantic, sweet—bring a few tears to the eyes of young and old.'

'Danny,' Shona teased, 'you're just an old sentimentalist at heart.'

'Don't mind me.' The voice came from behind them. 'I'm Joe, ship's electrician. I'll fix up the mike and so on. Okay?'

Shona had turned to see a slim, curly-haired young man, his eyes bright with enthusiasm for his work.

'You're a walking advertisement for job satisfaction, Joe,' Danny joked, plainly a friend of the young man's. Joe laughed and carried on working.

As the concert began, Shona sensed that from the start the audience were with them. In the large room people were grouped around tables and wine waiters drifted noiselessly from one to the other, taking and delivering orders.

Soon all drinking seemed to be suspended as Shona's playing and Danny's singing gripped them. The music swayed the audience, now with nostalgia, now back to the present with more modern rhythms. As the old romantic songs were played, middle-aged eyes grew moist with memories, wives' and husbands' bodies began to sway, not only with the ship's movement, but in an effort to catch at wispy fragments of their youth, hopes and dreams.

There was prolonged applause and as it died away Shona went to the microphone. 'Danny and I,' she said, her professional training overcoming her shyness, 'have composed between us a concerto for piano and guitar. We've called it the *Sea Wanderer* Concerto. There's nothing written down and it's all in our minds. And, if you'll forgive a touch of sentiment,' she gazed around, half-dazzled by the lighting which was directed at the platform, 'in our hearts, too. We give it to you as a memento of this cruise—with our love.'

As the applause rose and faded in expectation, Shona returned to her seat at the piano. Her heart had begun to thud as though someone had trodden hard on the loud pedal in her brain. Standing in the shadows, on the edge of the audience, she had seen Marsh Faraday.

Seeking for composure and serenity, she pushed everything from her mind but the music which was taking command of her. Raising her hands, she glanced at a waiting Danny and began to play.

Everything she had felt that morning as she had composed the music, every sound, thought and movement which she had translated into chords, harmonies and melodies flowed again from her brain. Bound together by her emotions, they reached deep into the hearts of her listeners, stirring them to the brink of tears.

As the concerto reached its climax—the parting of the ways at the end of the cruise—then died away, there was a moment's pause. When the applause finally broke out, it was rapturous and deafening.

Her hand extended towards Danny and together they bowed, acknowledging the ovation. People stood, stamped their feet, shouted 'More!' Danny looked at Shona questioningly, but she shook her head, too drained to perform again. Danny put down his guitar and hugged her to him, kissing her on the cheek. Again the audience responded. When the performers turned away the applause ended at last.

A drink was placed in Shona's hand and she drank it gladly. It helped just a little to revitalise her exhausted energies. 'Come and join the crowd?' Danny invited, but Shona said, 'Later, Danny, when I've been to my cabin.'

'I'll take you there,' he said, handing her the music they had used for the first part of the concert. He propped his guitar against a chair and together they made for the swing doors.

The electrician who, Shona assumed, had come to dismantle the various pieces of equipment, said, 'Great music you made,' and Shona thanked him. She would not allow herself to look for Marsh. He had probably left the Orchid Room long ago, possibly even in the middle of the performance.

With Danny at her side, Shona eased her way through the dispersing audience. There were calls of, 'Great, Miss Carroll,' and 'Congratulations. You, too, Danny.' Shona smiled and nodded her thanks and Danny lifted his hand.

As they passed through the exit doors, Shona felt the tight knot of tension inside her burst and open out like a flower to the sun. In lifting others to the heights of musical pleasure, she had risen to them herself.

The joy of achievement had put a brilliance into her eyes and a song in the pulsing of her heart. At last she had proved, to herself as well as others, that she possessed ability, even though it stopped short of Calvin's virtuosity.

It was as they were walking along the corridor near to the ship's offices that Calvin, with Toni following, met them and stood arms folded, blocking the way. His hair had fallen over his forehead, perspiration stood out on his upper lip. 'My God,' he said to Shona, 'what an unutterable cacophony of sound you made. And you had the cheek to call it the *Sea Wanderer* Concerto! People have been thrown overboard for less. And your playing—it was atrocious.' There was a supporting giggle from Toni. 'How you could sit there,' Calvin went on, 'in front of that gullible audience and hit those piano keys as though you were putting on a performance fit for royalty, without feeling a cheat and a hypocrite——!'

Shona went white and groped for support. Danny took her arm. 'Come on, Shona,' he urged. 'You haven't got to listen to this tin-whistle-blowing fool.'

Shona resisted Danny's tugs. 'It's all right, Danny. Calvin's clever. He's a brilliant flautist. He knows about music. If he says the concerto was rubbish, then it was rubbish. If he says I'm a terrible pianist, I'm a terrible pianist. I——'

her voice wavered, 'I just thought, for once, that I'd sur-passed my usual moderate performance and produced something worthwhile ...'

A sob escaped her control as the high barriers of her tension gave way. She sought somewhere, anywhere to hide her face, conceal the bitter tears that despite all her efforts, would come. Head down, hand to her face, she turned this way and that and found herself being hauled close to a granite-like wall, felt arms encompass her and lead her away. Her forehead found a place to rest beneath which was a thudding beat which brought memories of the storm sequence in the concerto.

She was urged round a corner. There were voices, a reply. 'Right, Mr Faraday. No, I don't mind at all. Ten minutes?' The door shut and Shona sensed she was alone with the man—she guessed his identity from the feel of his arms—who held her now with such gentleness that all her unhappiness, disappointment and worst of all, disillusion, flowed out with her tears.

After a while she was still, lying exhausted against him, conscious of a boundless strength which she wished she, too, possessed. 'I'm sorry,' she said, her voice hoarse, her lips dry. Her tear-reddened eyes lifted miserably to his.

'I'm your makebelieve lover, remember?' Marsh said softly, cupping her cheek and chin and trailing his lips across her other cheek to her ear. 'Shall I recap? We're having an affair, you and I, to bring your fiancé to heel. As your lover-by-adoption, certain rights have passed to me, like rescuing you from a carping, sniping fellow-profes-sional.'

'If you mean Calvin, he was right.'

Marsh stood apart from her. 'If that's how you see it——' his shrug finished the sentence. 'Come to my suite. I'll give you a drink.'

'Suite'. The word conjured up a setting to which, in her present dejected state, she would be completely unable to adjust. Simplicity was what her tortured feelings needed, quietness and a familiarity.

'Marsh,' she stroked the velvet of his bow tie—a touch of evening formality worn by many of the men passengers, 'mind if I go to my cabin instead?'

'Anywhere's better than here,' was his response as he looked around at filing cabinets, typewriters and folders bulging with paper.

At her cabin door, Marsh took her key and unfastened the lock, standing back to allow her access. She turned to thank him, but he indicated that he intended following. Walking across to the window, Shona parted the curtains which the steward had pulled across.

Behind her, the cabin was in darkness, but she had deliberately left it so. The door closed and she tensed, expecting a hand to touch her, but instead there was silence. Silence in which there was the constant engine-throb, like a steady, reassuring heartbeat, silence in which she could feel her muscle tautness ease, the blood pounding through her veins slow down, the tumult of aroused and angry passions soothed into a sighing acceptance of the truth.

The sea was calm, the ship's movement minimal. Lights from the lower decks shone upon the water and the reflected white ripples passed across the ceiling. It was as if she were alone, but Shona knew Marsh was there.

'Thanks,' she said after a while, 'for your understanding.' She faced him in the semi-darkness and saw that he was leaning on a shoulder against the door. 'And for giving me a shoulder to cry those tears on.'

His silence persisted.

'I couldn't help it, Marsh. I'd reached a high—you know, achievement, success, self-congratulations—only to have my bubble pricked until it burst in my face.' Again she watched the dancing lights on the sea. 'It hurt——'

'Coming from Calvin Faber?'

She nodded. 'He's no fool.'

'In his own line.'

Shona smiled wanly, turning and walking to the bed. 'I suppose you mean his little affair with Toni.' She shrugged and sat on the side of the bed. 'Rather now than after——'

After what? His ring was no longer in place on her finger. Did she ever want it to be there again?

Marsh strolled across to sit beside her, and she said, 'Musically he knows what he's talking about, even if he does occasionally get his women mixed up.'

'Has it happened before?'

Shona was growing conscious of Marsh's thigh pressing against hers. It confused her. 'I—I don't believe it has, to be honest. At home, he's too absorbed in his work. All day, every day, his musician friends come and go. They talk music and nothing but music.' She thought a moment. 'I don't mind, usually, because music's my life, too.'

'How did it happen that he asked you to marry him?'

'We share the house, five of us. Three men, two girls. The other girl's going to marry one of the other men. Calvin looked at me one day, realised I wasn't all that bad to look at——'

Marsh seized her chin, jerked it round and said, 'Are you blind, girl?'

Momentarily, her spirits revived, and she managed a smile. 'Don't soft-soap me, Mr Faraday.'

He released her chin and brushed it playfully with his fist. 'So it took another engagement to make him remember he was a man, too, with the male sex drive which, at times, needs pandering to. Which is how he uses you, when the fancy takes him?'

Shona was glad Marsh could not see the colour in her cheeks. She could not remember the last time Calvin had exhibited any 'sex drive' at all.

'Like you,' she said simply, and unknowingly revealing her secret thought, 'blondes turn him on.' A weariness overcame her and her body sagged. An arm crept round her, pulling her to him. A hand went up and buried itself in her hair. Fingers tightened and there was a tug which was almost a wordless order. Her head tipped back obediently and a mouth took hers.

The kiss was a taking and a giving. Eagerly Shona responded, reaching out to the proffered solace, drawing into

her body some of that strength which had earlier given her
support and consolation. When Marsh pressed her back
until she lay full-length on the bed, she did not stiffen.
When he eased himself beside her, she made room for him
gladly.

'What are you doing,' he murmured against her ear,
'using me to escape from those terrible inadequacies your
boy-friend threw at you after the concert?' His hand found
her breast, caressing it with a possession she did not question. 'Are you,' he went on, and she heard him through the
sea-mist of delight in which his fondling was enfolding her,
'rationalising away your audacity, as you no doubt now
think of it, in presenting yourself to that very receptive
audience tonight as an accomplished musician?'

'Oh, Marsh,' she rolled on to her side, 'I don't know.
When—when you do this to me, I can't think, I can only
feel. Marsh,' she was in a half-waking, half-dreaming state
now, 'you don't have to stay. You've calmed me down,
you've——'

'*Calmed* you,' he remarked, finding her wrist and testing it, 'you call yourself calm when your pulse is throbbing,
and,' his hand moved to her ribs, 'your heart's racing? If
this is what I do to you, what better way to escape from
your problems than letting me love you?'

He found the neckline of her dress, slid it downwards
until the silky softness he was seeking gleamed in the
semi-darkness. His lips on the enticing roundness had her
arching toward him and whispering his name.

Then she remembered—this man was play-acting, it was
a makebelieve affair. But there was no audience to play to!
'Marsh,' she gasped, 'please, I never meant you to go this
far——'

There were voices outside. A voice that was Toni's
said, on a giggling note, 'I dare you to knock.'

'Dare? I'm her fiancé.' Calvin's voice was faintly
slurred. 'I could walk in, just like this.'

The door handle moved and Shona's lips parted in a

soundless gasp. Marsh's hand came up and covered her mouth.

'Damn,' said Calvin's voice. 'It's locked.' Shona relaxed, putting her hand over Marsh's and it was as though her lips were kissing his palm. 'Is she in or out?'

'In stupid,' Toni mumbled. 'She's probably weeping, big silent tears because of the way you spoke to her.' There was a foolish laugh.

'She's stupid,' said Calvin, knocking on the door. 'So's that rubbish she dreamed up.'

'Danny helped,' Toni pointed out. 'He was good. I think the music was good.' The voices were fading, a key was turning. 'You're just a musical snob, Calvin Faber.'

'Come on in,' Calvin invited. 'Give me what my too-too-superior fiancée won't. That's why I like you. You're not mean with your kisses, or your——' The cabin door snapped shut, the lock was turned.

'Marsh.' Shona's head turned and her cheek pressed against his. He had become so familiar to her now. How often had they kissed, touched? That morning in the pool, when they had been so close it was almost as if they were one. Now here they were lying together ... 'Why must it only be makebelieve love, Marsh?' She snuggled against him, putting her arm across his waist. 'I want you to make love to me, Marsh. I know it means leaving the "love" out, but,' she pressed her face to the muscular elasticity of his waist, 'I can't say "make passion to me," can I?'

Her head rose and fell with his breathing. He had neither responded nor answered. She uncurled a little and gazed up at him. In the light that danced on the ceiling, his face looked as if it was carved in stone. 'Why are you looking so far away, Marsh?' she asked in a small voice, snuggling against him again.

After a few moments he eased her from his side and rested on an elbow. Carefully he pulled her dress back into place and Shona felt a wave of embarrassment sweep over her. Yet she had no regrets about having allowed Marsh to kiss her and gentle her so intimately.

'A few minutes ago,' she whispered, gazing at a blurred shadow that was now his face, 'you tried to persuade me to let you love me. Marsh, don't you understand? Now I'm *asking* you.'

'My sweet,' he answered dryly, 'that's only too clear. If I asked you "why", what would you say?'

'Because I—I——' 'Want you', would she answer? Need you? *Love* you? Only the last would suffice and he wouldn't believe it.

His head lowered to the pillow and he pulled her to him. 'Shona, my makebelieve love, I'll not be any man's stand-in when it comes to making love to a woman. Nor am I a thief-in-the-night, day or any other time. It's against my principles to steal another man's woman.'

He buttoned his shirt from which he had removed the bow tie. 'Marsh,' her hand caught his arm, 'please stay——' She was caught by a shaking, shivering yawn and he laughed softly.

'Nor would an emotionally exhausted woman be any good to me.'

'Marsh,' she lay limply watching him as he rose and pulled on his jacket, 'how can you be so unfeeling?'

'Unfeeling, she calls me!' He leaned over her, a hand on her pillow, the other turning her head. His mouth found hers and her arms reached up to lock round his neck. As they kissed, her desires stirred and she clung even tighter. 'Oh, no, my sweet.' He pulled her arms away. 'That was not a prelude to a night of love. That was to demonstrate that I've got feelings and to show just how inflamed they are. It was also,' from the door, 'goodnight. We dock in the morning at Las Palmas. I'll see you then.'

CHAPTER SEVEN

'THERE'S no performance this evening.' Calvin stood near the door of Shona's cabin. 'Did I remember to tell you?'

'For once, you did.' Shona was inspecting her white tee-shirt and pale blue slacks in the wall mirror. 'You never told me the programme schedule for the cruise.' She tightened the white belt. 'I just await my daily instructions from my partner, the world-famous flute player—or get them from the ship's newspaper which the cabin steward puts on the tea tray every morning.'

'You can keep your sarcasm for the shipping company director,' Calvin snapped.

'You can talk.' She faced him. 'What sort of a night did you have with your new girl-friend? Did she come up with the goods—to your *entire* satisfaction?'

'So you were in here after all? Why didn't you open the door when I knocked? Hey, what's this?'

Shona turned and saw the object in his hand. It was the black velvet bow tie Marsh had been wearing when he had brought her to her cabin. She turned quickly away to hide her consternation. Forcing her voice to be casual, she answered,

'It's a tie, it's made of velvet——'

'And it's Marsh Faraday's.'

She confronted him. 'So what if it is? If you can entertain another woman in your cabin, what's to stop me entertaining a man in mine?'

'And did you "entertain" him?' She was silent but smiling tormentingly. 'Look, you're my fiancée, Shona. Doesn't that mean anything to you?'

'As much as it means to you which, judging by your blossoming new relationship, is nothing. Why should there be one law for you and another for me? Anyway, Marsh was kind to me after you upset me——'

'Kind, was he?' Calvin was near to losing his temper.

'Yes, very.' The voice came from behind them. 'I gave her exactly what she needed. And I'll have my tie back, please. Thanks.' He pushed the tie into his pocket. 'She didn't answer the door because I was so busy being kind to her. A little'—he glanced at Shona—'love goes a long way when a woman's upset. But that's something you'll learn when you grow up.'

'Why, you——' Calvin swung a fist. Even if Marsh hadn't ducked, the blow would have missed wildly. 'Keep your miserable hands off her, understand?'

'Even if she invites me to put my hands *on* her?'

'You know what you are?' Calvin came back. 'A rotten, low-down——'

'I could have your contract with Ocean Rover Shipping Company cancelled at the lift of that telephone, Mr Faber.'

'Then she'd suffer, wouldn't she?' Calvin sneered.

'And,' as if he had not spoken, 'in its place give a contract to Miss Carroll to supply the classical music for the rest of the cruise. I could also have you put off the ship here in Las Palmas, which means you'd have to find your own way home at your own expense.' Calvin's colour was so high Shona grew worried. 'But I won't,' Marsh went on, 'out of kindness to your fiancée. And for your information, I didn't spend the night with her.'

Calvin's muscles visibly slackened.

'Only part of it.' Marsh was smiling.

Calvin said to Shona, 'I'm not sitting with you on the outing this morning.'

'That's just as well,' Marsh put in, 'because I've already made arrangements for you to sit elsewhere. With Toni Hardy, in another coach.'

Calvin stormed out and Shona sank, hand to head, on to a chair. 'Men,' she mumbled, 'I *hate* them!'

'So I've noticed,' Marsh commented dryly. 'Come on, we're going down to breakfast.'

*

With Marsh beside her in the luxury coach, it was difficult to take in the scenery which flashed past the windows. They had driven through Las Palmas and seen in the parks and lining the streets, clusters of towering palm trees, their long leaves throwing sun-shadows all around.

The coach passed hotel blocks and buildings of industry and commerce, driving on through the old quarter of the city where, the courier informed them, there were buildings going back to the *conquistadores*. There were narrow, balconied streets, peaceful plazas and ancient churches, all of which seemed to have escaped the ravages of the passing centuries.

As they drove towards the countryside Shona noticed how abundantly the palm trees grew. This, Marsh told her, was how the city they had just left behind had got its name, as the Spanish for palm trees was 'Las Palmas'.

There were hairpin bends with steep drops to one side and Shona held her breath at the sight of them. At the final bend, the fall away of the land to the right of the coach was spectacular. There, Marsh pointed, was the crater of an extinct volcano. Far below, at the bottom of the crater, there were green and brown areas of farmed land, and even a farmhouse, and a cluster of buildings.

A stop was made at a small shop selling souvenirs and handicrafts. A young woman took Shona's hand and sprayed perfume on it, indicating that she should inhale its scent. Marsh, too, breathed in its fragrance, kissing Shona's palm before releasing her wrist. The young woman was delighted at the act, and pointed to a picture of the Bird of Paradise flower, indicating that this was its source.

When the girl, in broken English, quoted the price, Shona shook her head, but Marsh, addressing her in Spanish, bought a large bottle and presented it to Shona. The young woman's face was wreathed in smiles and spoke rapidly in Spanish to Marsh. As they left the shop, Shona asked him what she had said.

'She wished us every happiness,' he said, smiling wickedly as Shona turned pink at the implication.

'That's two things you've bought me,' she told him as they settled down in the coach again.

'Your debts are mounting, my girl,' he said with mock fierceness. 'Soon I shall demand payment in kisses—plus.'

Verity Faraday, who sat behind them with John Victor, laughed. 'Heed the gypsy's warning, Shona. Beware the man who piles gifts upon you. For "man", read "my son".' As her son turned a threatening face towards her, Verity laughed, 'I can see I'm treading on delicate ground. I'm being told to keep off my son's love life.'

The tour continued through an exciting countryside of palm trees and exotic flowers, the deep green of the banana plantations in the valleys contrasting strongly with awesome mountain peaks.

The coach driver stopped for refreshments at a building with a wooden exterior. This led to a damp, winding and unlighted tunnel. Rock jutted from the sides and top and Shona clung to Marsh's hand, baffled by the darkness and worried by the slippery dampness underfoot.

They emerged into a room which had been created by volcanic lava and had been made, incredibly, into a restaurant. Through the windows along one wall, there were breathtaking views of the surrounding mountains. Drinks were taken in a café and outside were lemon and orange trees holding tiny formations of the growing fruit.

Arriving back at the ship, Marsh stood back to allow Shona to precede him upwards along the gangway. The air-conditioned coolness was welcome after the heavy warmth of the air outside.

Marsh detained Shona. 'This evening, will you come for a walk in the city?'

Shona tried to disguise her pleasure at the invitation. 'Maybe,' she answered, hoping she sounded offhand. A playful slap and a menacing, 'You will,' sent her on her way.

After lunch, Shona changed into a blue and white striped two-piece swimsuit. Since the sky was a little overcast, she pulled on a white cotton skirt and a short matching jacket.

It was difficult in the controlled coolness of the ship to guess the temperature outside.

There were only a scattering of people around the pool, so it seemed that many passengers had gone ashore. Calvin reclined in a deck chair. His swimming trunks were dry and he wore an unbuttoned shirt. Although at first he appeared to be sleeping, his eyes were open.

As Shona studied him she experienced no feeling of attraction at all. He saw her and, after a significant pause, raised his hand and let it fall. It seemed to indicate that he did not care greatly whether she joined him or not. A sense of obligation took her to his side.

'Is this anybody's?' She indicated the empty chair next to his.

A shoulder moved carelessly. 'Toni's rehearsing a show for this evening. She won't be back.'

Shona sank down, dropping her towel. She inspected the sky. 'I hope the sun comes through soon.'

'Yes.'

A moment's thought gave Shona the next verbal move. 'Enjoying the cruise?'

'So-so.'

'Oh.' Two minutes' consideration provided another subject. 'Did you like this morning's tour?'

'It was okay.'

'I enjoyed it very much.'

'That's fine, then.'

If he carries on like this, Shona told herself, I'll throw something at him. Her eyes were drawn involuntarily to her left. A smiling, watching face looked back at her from a nearby deckchair. So Marsh had overheard their scintillating conversation. His body and trunks, she noticed, were damp. Unlike Calvin, he had used the pool. Abruptly, Shona stood up, peeled off her jacket and skirt and stood, arms stretched, free of all cover but her brief swimming outfit. She looked down at Calvin. He watched her moodily. She looked at Marsh. He was watching, narrow-eyed.

Shona knew what he was thinking—that she was again

revelling in her male audience—but she simply didn't care. If she could, she thought, she would have banged their two heads together. Since they were both so interested in her, she would give them something to look at. There was a single-platform diving board and Shona climbed on to it, stood, arms stretched and leapt.

It was a long way short of a perfect dive and as she curved upwards to the surface, she shook the water from her eyes and saw, to her annoyance, that Calvin's eyes were closed again and that Marsh was smiling broadly.

Other people were splashing around her, shouting to each other. Watching them, she felt lonely. 'Calvin,' she called, 'come on in!'

Without even opening his eyes, he shook his head. Angry now, she called 'Marsh?' He smiled a little, which was the only answer she received from him. She fought off the feeling of humiliation and put her back to them, curving and submerging and swimming under water until she was forced to surface for air.

When she decided she had had enough she climbed the steps out of the pool to find a pair of tough male legs, slightly apart, an arm's stretch from where she paused. Thighs with muscles like whipcord supported hard-boned hips and, above the clip-buckled trunks a tanned body led to broad shoulders and an arrogantly-held head which, at that moment, was tilted forward to watch her breathless progress up the steps.

'You called me,' he remarked. 'Here I am.' It was his smile that annoyed her.

'Please let me pass.' Although the sun was making an effort to penetrate the cloud, it was cool and she shivered.

'When you've told me what you wanted.'

'Oh,' she hoped her careless tone would suffice. 'It doesn't matter now.' His intimidating body stayed right where it was. She forced out a sigh. 'Company, that's all.'

'And when your fiancé wouldn't oblige——' Shona shushed him in case Calvin heard, 'he's gone,' Marsh supplied blandly, and continued, 'you wanted me as a substitute and also as a weapon to make Faber jealous.' Marsh moved aside and Shona climbed the last two steps.

His eyes ran appreciatively over her scantily-clad form, lingering with knowing eyes on the fullness of her beasts, every detail of which the wet triangles of the bra top revealed.

'Yes to both,' she answered, hoping to irritate him back, 'and why not? We made an agreement——'

'We did, one crazy midnight.'

'A promise that you'd help me get—get Calvin back.' And now I don't want him, her thoughts intervened. I only want you.

'What do I get out of it?' His hands fisted on his hips and at the sight of his aggressive demeanour Shona's heart tilted and righted like a toy with a rounded base.

'Kisses.' She looked up at him, smiling. He shook his head, implying that was not enough, but she could not put into words the other familiarities she had allowed him.

'I want more than that.' The sun burst free of the cloud and flooded the ship from stem to stern. 'Before we're finished, Miss Shona Carroll, I'll take what I want from you, and to hell with what's left for Calvin Faber.'

'Marsh,' her hand gripped his arm, her face looked momentarily pale in the gold light of the sun, 'you can't.'

His head thrust forward, his eyes, already in shadow, darkened. 'Challenging me, lady? If you do, we'll see who's the stronger.' Without a second's warning, his fist hit her shoulder and she fell backwards into the pool, gasping with the sharpness of the impact.

'You're a hard, unfeeling savage!' she shouted at him, but he laughed, hands on hips.

'Remember our evening in Las Palmas,' he called, and walked purposefully away.

It was as dusk was falling that Shona found herself climbing down iron steps from the side of the ship and jumping into a small launch that bobbed vigorously in the water. Lights from the shore glinted and swirled with the muted movement of the waves, giving the city an aura of romance.

The launch was crowded and Marsh, beside her, put his arm about her, tucking her into his side. Calvin, who sat across from them, stared, then glared as Shona responded to the tricks the pressure of Marsh's body was playing on her nervous system. She did nothing to hide the warmth in her eyes as she gazed up at the man at her side, replying with a tremulous smile as he looked down at her.

A swift frown pleated his forehead and Shona knew it was a warning to her not to overact. She wished she could tell him, I don't care what Calvin thinks. It's you I love, it never has been Calvin. But even if they had been alone, she knew how impossible it would have been for her to have spoken the words. Marsh would have dismissed them with a cynical smile, as he had no doubt dismissed the two women to whom he had once been engaged.

The launch sped across the water, racing through the dancing, reflected shore lights to the mainland. The launch tied up at a jetty and its passengers disembarked. A handful of people climbed out, many of them members of the ship's crew. Then Marsh took a deep step upwards and turned to help Shona. His arms gripped her waist and he swung her from the rocking boat to stand beside him on the stone steps. Calvin was talking to a young man whom Shona recognised as being a member of the entertainments crew.

Marsh took Shona's hand and she made no complaint at his unexpectedly possessive attitude. If Calvin objected, why should she care? She did not even look back to see if he was following. They crossed a busy street and walked past shops with closed doors where men lounged, watching passers-by.

Flashing lights in red, yellow or white announced the presence of bars, nightclubs and places to dance. Marsh led Shona on, his arm now across her shoulders, until they reached a paved square. In the centre a fountain was illuminated from below and the cascading water looked almost silver against the darkness.

There was a bench nearby and Marsh indicated with a tug that he intended occupying it. They sat, side by side, and long, firm fingers found her chin, urging it round, tipping her head and holding it ready for the kiss they both knew was coming.

'Marsh,' Shona whispered urgently, 'Calvin might see.'

'We lost him back there,' was the impatient answer. An equally impatient mouth covered Shona's, turning hard and compelling, forcing hers to open and allow his probing kiss access to the honey hers contained. A hand lifted and fastened, with an ungentle action, on the shapely fullness that pressed against her silky summer top.

When his head lifted, at last, leaving his hand in undisputed possession of her pouting femininity, Shona whispered, in a puzzled voice, 'Marsh—why? Calvin's not here to see, so——?'

'Isn't it only human,' his eyes dropped to where his hand was resting so comfortably, 'for a man who's doing a woman a favour to expect a reward? I warned you, my sweet, that I'd want repayment, and heaven knows, this is little enough.'

'Oh, Marsh,' her voice was soft and her eyes dancing in the lights of the cascading fountain, 'if you knew how much I've been wanting you to kiss me——'

'To spite your fiancé? I'm aware of that.' His tone was dry and a little edged.

If she shook her head, he would only laugh. He was a cynic on the subject of women. Wasn't that plain from all he'd said about them? Nevertheless her hand moved to cover his as it held her, pressing it closer, asking silently for more—and more.

He laughed and eased her away, moving his hand to grasp hers and pull her up. 'Too public, Shona. Wait until we're in the privacy of my cabin—or yours. You make the choice.'

She jerked from him and walked apart. 'You make it sound sordid,' she snapped, glad that he could not see the quick moistening of her eyes.

His arm captured her again. 'Love is never sordid.'

'But it wouldn't be love, would it?' He did not answer. 'Would it?' she repeated, wanting—longing for—an answer. She was to remain disappointed.

They were approaching a large open-air café. Most tables were occupied and Shona, looking for familiar faces, saw Calvin and the young man to whom he had spoken earlier. She recalled that he was the drummer in the band in which Danny played and sang.

There were two empty seats at their table and Marsh gestured, saying, 'Shall we?' He was distant now. There had been no physical contact between them since they had left the bench in the square.

The young man said, 'Hi.' He introduced himself as Ricky Timson. Calvin nodded, glancing sourly at Shona and Marsh. At arms' length he studied his empty beer glass. Marsh signalled to the waiter, ordered a beer for himself and a dry Martini for Shona. She thanked him and looked around, listening to the incessant chatter in many different languages, hearing the swish of passing traffic, and seeing in the darkness the lights of the cafés casting a silver glow on the surrounding palm trees.

A crowd of young people came trailing along the street, stopping beside the café. One of the young men carried a guitar and he spoke to his friends. Four of them broke away and formed a group near to the table where Shona sat. The guitar strings responded to the young man's fingers and to his accompaniment, three voices sang a plaintive Spanish song.

Calvin held his head. 'The guitarist should at least have taken lessons,' he groaned, 'before playing in public. Not to mention,' he saw a girl break away from the group's friends and hold out a cap to the café's patrons, 'expecting to be paid for an atrocious performance.'

Shona glanced at Marsh, but his face was unreadable. She hoped the young Spaniards could not understand English. Calvin, however, had no such scruples. It seemed he expected them to understand him when he spoke. As the song ended and the scattering of applause died down, he called out, 'You've got a cheek to ask for money for that shocking noise.'

The young man smiled, believing the words to be praise. Calvin, more irritated now, stood up. Agitatedly, Shona urged, 'No, Calvin, just let it be. He was doing his best.'

Calvin ignored her and confronted the young man. 'I'll play that,' he said, holding out his hand, 'I'll show you how.' The young man seemed puzzled. 'That guitar,' Calvin insisted, 'I'll play.'

The young man beamed and nodded and, to Shona's astonishment, handed over his guitar. Calvin ran experimental fingers over the strings, made a face at the lack of tone and picked out the simple tune of a nursery rhyme. The young man stood patiently for a few moments, then began to look worried. Irritation soon followed and he said, holding out his hand, 'Money, now.'

Calvin frowned. 'Who said anything about money?'

'You pay,' the guitarist insisted, 'you pay. You said.'

Realisation dawned and Calvin laughed. 'I said I'd play, not pay. Me, pay for *this*?' His distasteful expression was sufficient to cross all language barriers.

Incensed, the young man grabbed the guitar, but Calvin's hold tightened. 'I haven't finished yet,' he said imperiously, but it seemed the young man's knowledge of English was too small to comprehend his meaning.

Shona jumped up and tried to explain to the guitarist. 'He said he'd *play*,' she mimed the strumming action, 'not pay money.' She pretended to take coins from her pocket and brush them away. The young Spaniard shook his head, then began to tug his instrument from Calvin's stiffened fingers.

'Let go, you fool,' Calvin snarled, 'I won't be long.'

'For heaven's sake,' Shona begged, 'give him back his guitar, and let's go.'

Two young men detached themselves from the crowd on the pavement and swooped on Shona, holding her by the arms. Grinning, they began to drag her backwards into the dark café and she screamed. 'Marsh! Please do something. Stop Calvin——'

Calvin threw the guitar on to a table and pushed his way after his shrieking fiancée and her would-be abductors. The guitar's owner followed, swung Calvin round and punched him full on the mouth. The young men, pleased with their friend's act of retribution, let Shona go.

Her hands went to her cheeks and she gasped, 'He's a musician. He plays a flute. How can he play now?'

Marsh, who had been watching the episode, his eyes half closed, yet with his apparently indolent body tensing for action should it become necessary, stood up and spoke in rapid Spanish to the young guitarist. He took out his wallet, extracted a handful of Spanish money and handed it over.

Pleased with themselves, the crowd moved away, calling out to Calvin who was trying with a handkerchief to stem the flow of blood from his rapidly swelling lips. Their comments were plainly uncomplimentary, for the other customers laughed loudly. Marsh smiled, but his eyes were grim.

He reached out and gripped Shona's wrist. His hold was hardly less painful than the young men's had been. 'For God's sake, girl, keep your fiancé in order. He's surly, petulant and the most selfish male I've ever come across. Isn't it time you started giving him what's missing in his life? No wonder he turns to another woman at the snap of her fingers.'

'Let go of me!' Shona snapped, her eyes blazing. 'And keep your miserable insults to yourself. How Calvin and I conduct our relationship is none of your business. Anyway, look at him. He's in trouble. He needs help. Instead of standing there trying to humiliate me, can't you *do* something?'

Marsh's eyes grew hard. 'You insult *me*, young woman, and you'll find yourself across my knee. And the next time I give you a good spanking, it won't be in a public place like the swimming pool, but in privacy.'

Before she could reply, he had left her and had disappeared into the café, the interior of which had seemed earlier, when she was being dragged towards it, to be so frightening. When Marsh emerged, Shona was standing with her arm across Calvin's shoulders. He was slumped in a chair, the handkerchief still held to his mouth.

'Marsh,' said Shona, 'it won't stop bleeding.'

'I've called a taxi,' Marsh answered coolly. 'Here it is, in fact. Come on, Faber—or do you need help with walking?'

Calvin's eyes expressed the anger which his injured lips could not. He shook off Shona's helping hand and walked unsteadily to the cab. As they entered the ship, the hands of the clock reached midnight.

Marsh said, 'You know where the doctor's surgery is, Shona?' His voice, like his manner, was aloof. Shona nodded. 'Over to you, then,' said Marsh, and went on his way.

The doctor had given Calvin some sleeping pills, which he took with reluctance. He didn't want any medicine, he said, that would dull the brightness of his brain.

'Since you won't be playing the flute for a few days, Mr Faber,' the doctor had said dryly, 'the "brightness" of your brain can safely be allowed to grow a little dimmer for a night or so.'

'But I've got to play,' Calvin had protested. 'I'm here on a contract with the shipping company——'

'As someone else on a contract with the company, Mr Faber,' the doctor had answered, 'I can tell you that, in situations like this, Ocean Rover directors are very understanding. To put it bluntly, you'll get your money. Now, I think a good night's sleep will do you good, so I suggest you go to your cabin and retire to bed.' With which verbal pat on the head, the doctor saw Calvin and Shona to the door.

Next morning Shona drank her morning tea quickly, washed and dressed with equal speed and tapped on Calvin's door. There was no reply, so she went in search of the

cabin steward who unlocked Calvin's door for her. The
steward told her he knew about her fiancé's injury and had
left the tray of tea, hoping that he would be able to help
himself.

'I'll look after him, thanks,' said Shona with a sweet smile
which promptly faded when she saw Calvin's swollen
mouth and Calvin's black expression.

'It's about time,' he mumbled through puffy lips.
'Thought you were never coming. And don't you dare give
me that tea! I had an argument with the steward when he
tried to force me to drink it.'

Shona told herself to count to ten. Calvin was behaving
no differently from anyone with such an affliction as he
had. All the same, she found it hard to feel real sympathy
for him, since he had brought it on himself. But he had
tried to rescue her from those two young men ... Although
she doubted if they had had any evil intentions towards
her.

She sat on his bed and leaned across to kiss his cheek,
but he pulled back in horror. 'For God's sake,' he said
hoarsely, 'don't yearn for physical contact when I'm in this
state.'

Shona blushed and stood up. 'If that's your attitude, I'll
see you at breakfast.'

'Shona!' There was a little-boy appeal in his voice she
could not turn from. 'I can't come to breakfast looking like
this. Anyway, how could I eat? And I'm sorry if I snapped.
You would, too, if you'd been punched right here.' He indicated his mouth.

'Calvin, you're not an invalid. All right, so you've got a
sore mouth, but you could eat soft foods, drink cold milk.'

'I can't appear in public looking like this.' It was a
statement, and it was not to be challenged. 'Stay with me,
darling,' he wheedled. 'We are engaged, after all.'

'Are we?' Shona asked bitterly, adding, 'So you think I
should start my wifely duties right now by waiting on you
hand and foot——' She stopped, asking aghast, 'You're not
staying in bed all day?'

'Yes, I am. The doctor said I needed rest.'

It was a fact she could not dispute, though she felt sure that he had meant rest overnight, not all day as well. For most of that day she was kept a virtual prisoner in Calvin's cabin. His needs were endless, likewise his demands.

She had her breakfast and even her lunch with him, although she insisted that during the afternoon she would have to find the entertainments manager and tell him the concert scheduled for that evening could not take place.

Leaving Calvin, she walked stealthily as though she was escaping from prison, afraid that Calvin would jump out of bed and drag her back. She found herself running to the lift—and collided with another person. Two arms encircled her and they felt so familiar she wanted to cry.

'Why the hurry?' the drawling male voice asked.

'Oh, Marsh!' Her cheek rested against him, her arms lifted to find his waist. It was only at that moment that she realised just how tired she was. When a finger hooked under her chin and lifted her face, there was a trace of tears —of fatigue, not sorrow.

'Come on', his arm went round her and he led her to the lift. He told the bellboy, 'W deck, please,' and Shona knew he was taking her to his cabin.

The elegance and luxury which had hit her on her first visit there went unnoticed by her dulled brain. He led her to the couch and she lay back on the cushions, letting her head fall to one side and closing her eyes.

'Drink?' Marsh asked, but she murmured, 'No, thanks.' She heard footsteps, the chink of glasses, liquid being poured. The footsteps moved to the expanse of window behind her and Marsh stood, contemplating the swell of the sea. 'Homeward-bound,' he commented, and Shona's heart sank like a boat in a storm.

'There's Gibraltar first,' she mumbled, thinking of anything, any barrier to erect between their existing strange involvement and its fast-approaching and inevitable end.

'Yes,' he said, his back still to her, 'there's Gib.' With the extra sensitivity which tiredness seemed to have given her, Shona perceived that there was a great deal more in his thoughts than in his words. She was invaded by a curious feeling of anxiety, but she brushed it aside as worry about Calvin, and her immediate problems, took over.

She twisted on the couch and curled her legs under her, looking at Marsh's broad back. 'This evening, Marsh?' He made a movement, indicating that she had his attention. 'The concert—it'll have to be cancelled. Calvin won't be in a condition to play——'

'But *you* will.' The quiet words had her staring. Slowly he turned, glass in hand, his unwavering gaze fastening upon her.

Her hand pointed to herself. She shook her head wildly. 'Not me, not on my own. I can't, Marsh,' she pleaded, 'so please don't make me. I'm here as an accompanist, a *substitute* accompanist, not a solo pianist.' His eyes did not soften, they hardened. He put down his glass. 'I'd be afraid, Marsh,' she whispered. 'A completely solo performance would be entirely outside my experience.'

He stood in front of her. 'Isn't it time you acknowledged that you're a better performing artist than you think? Hasn't it ever occurred to you that you've been brainwashed by that *brilliantly gifted* fiancé of yours?'

She stiffened at the sarcastic emphasis of the last phrase.

'That he's persuaded you into accepting,' Marsh went on relentlessly, 'that you're not just second-rate, but third and even fourth-rate as a musician?'

Shona said, staring at the gold-coloured carpet, 'That old lady told me she thought I was a better performer than Calvin.'

'Which shows what excellent perception she's got. I've heard similar comments from your audiences while sitting amongst them.'

Shona shook her head. 'They're wrong. Technically, Calvin's brilliant——'

'Good grief,' Marsh sat beside her, 'he's been even more successful in hypnotising you into accepting his so-called superiority than I thought.'

She leaned back wearily, closing her eyes. 'He is superior. All the critics say he's near-genius.'

'Have the critics ever heard you?'

'Me?' Her eyes flew open, then closed. She smiled. 'You have to be joking! I'm a music teacher, one of the back-room people who bring out the best in others——'

'And constantly hold back on their own abilities for fear of swamping those of their pupils.'

Her head slipped a little towards him. 'You're very kind, Marsh, but I think I understand why you're trying to boost my courage. Someone has to entertain those people this evening——'

His hand fastened round her throat and he shifted until he hovered over her, his face menacingly close. His eyes were like a storm-tossed sea as his mouth bore down, taking hers in a punishing kiss. His fingers tightened and she dared not struggle in case he deprived her completely of the power to breathe. When at last his head lifted, she lay there bruised and bewildered, gazing up at him, vulnerable and weak with longing—for his tenderness and his love.

His expression grew more gentle and he smiled. 'I should have remembered my maxim—never attempt to arouse a woman who's tired beyond words.'

'It's Calvin, Marsh.' Her voice wavered. 'He's made so many demands on me. He pleaded with me to stay with him, eat with him and be within call all day.'

Marsh's jaw clamped tight. 'The selfish swine!' When Shona's head turned from him, he turned it back, seeing the glint of tears. He gathered her into his arms, pulled her head to rest on his shoulder and sat thus until, entirely against her will, she fell asleep.

When Shona awoke, Marsh was standing beside the couch where she lay full-length. His eyes swept her, a smile lingering.

'As soon as I take my arms away and leave you, you wake up looking as though you want me back.' Shona rubbed her eyes and smiled up at him, seeing his shirt opened to the waist revealing the dark hairs against which she was sure her cheek had nestled. 'And looking,' he added, 'as though you want a "good morning" kiss when it's four o'clock in the afternoon.'

He ran fingers through his untidy hair and swallowed the drink he held.

She sat up. 'It can't be!'

'It is. And look at you, you wanton hussy. You look as though you've let a man do what he wanted with you.' He put down his glass with a clatter.

She blushed and glanced down. Her tee-shirt had worked upwards, exposing her midriff, as if a man's hand ... In her dream, a man who had had Marsh's compelling eyes, long sweep of jaw and full, determined mouth, had whispered endearments, stroked her body into surrender, into clinging, delighted submission.

'Marsh,' her large eyes held his, 'you didn't——'

His hand found his own heart. 'I swear that I didn't. But not for want of encouragement.'

'Oh, Marsh, I was asleep.'

'Ah, but what sweet dreams you had.' He held out his hand. 'Come with your dream lover, Shona Carroll, and we'll freshen up that brain of yours by a brisk walk around the deck.'

Arms round each other, uncaring who saw them, they walked in the fresh breeze, passing passengers who smiled, crew members who looked at Marsh with respect, junior officers who saluted briefly.

Shona glanced up at the man against whose side she snuggled. 'Going around with you makes me feel important.'

'Social climber!' Marsh accused, and kissed her upturned mouth.

'Playing for high stakes, Shona?' Toni's voice held a sneer. She watched with satisfaction while Shona reddened. 'How's Cal?'

'When I left Calvin about an hour and a half ago,' Shona answered levelly, 'he was playing the irritable, hard-done-by invalid to perfection. And slowly driving me mad in the process. Why did you want to know, Toni?'

'I thought I'd call in on him. I haven't before because I didn't want to interrupt—anything.' She feigned a smile. 'But I did, didn't I?' She stole a look at Marsh. 'With another man. A case of kissing someone else's lips while your own lover's are out of action.'

'Think what you like,' Shona retorted, 'and Calvin too!' She grasped Marsh's hand and pulled him after her. 'And,' she called over her shoulder, 'Calvin's *not* my lover.'

'That's what he said,' Toni shouted back. 'Poor man, he told me how you keep him at arms' length.'

Shona turned to answer, but found Marsh's hand covering her mouth. 'Let her have the last word. The cruise will be over soon, and everything between you and your fiancé will be back to normal.'

Shona was silent, but she wanted to scream out that she no longer had any feelings for the man everyone called her fiancé—if she'd ever had any feelings for him in the past. That it was he, Marsh Faraday, she wanted, above all other men.

'Marsh,' she said as they reached the stern and leaned on the barrier to watch the streaming, foaming wash of the ship. 'I'm not afraid about this evening any more. I had a wonderful dream——'

'I'll say you did,' was the amused reply, 'and did *I* enjoy it, too!'

Shona turned pink. 'I'm sure you're exaggerating. Anyway, the dream I'm talking about is where I played and played and the whole audience rose to their feet, clapping me. They shouted for more and even then they weren't satisfied. It was in the—Royal Festival Hall, I think.'

Marsh's laugh rang out across the sea's rolling expanse. 'Modest, aren't we?' he remarked.

Shona frowned. 'One of these days,' it was a promise half to herself, 'I'll be taken seriously as a pianist. One day ...'

*

Calvin's cabin door was open when Shona returned. Toni was sitting on his bed. It looked as if the place was not unfamiliar to her.

'Shona?' Calvin called. She stood in the doorway. 'About this evening—Toni said there'll be an announcement apologising for cancelling the concert.'

'No need to make any announcement.' She directed her words at Toni. 'I'm playing solo. We can't let the faithful down.'

Toni looked incredulous. 'But Calvin said you couldn't carry an audience on your own, even an uncritical one like the cruise passengers.'

'You *can't* play,' Calvin stated, 'not without a supporting performer.'

'Have a bet with me?' asked Shona, her whole body a challenge.

'Okay, have it your way,' Calvin answered badtemperedly. 'But don't burst into tears when they start talking amongst themselves and when it gets so loud, you can't hear yourself play.'

'Isn't there a very old saying,' Shona commented oversweetly, ' "the show must go on"?' She swung away to her cabin.

As she went down in the lift to the restaurant, Shona thought about Calvin's pleading with her to have her evening meal with him. When she had replied firmly that she was dressing for dinner and joining the others at their usual table, he had reproached her loudly for deserting him in his hour of need.

When she told him that apart from a bruised mouth there was nothing wrong with him, and that there was therefore no reason why he shouldn't come, too, he answered spitefully that he hoped she made such a mess of the solo performance that she'd never have the cheek to perform alone in public again.

The lift doors opened. Over the heads of the passengers who emerged she saw in front of her the tall figure of Marsh Faraday. Her heart began to hammer, but she knew that he was waiting for his mother. She could not believe, even when his hand grasped her wrist, that he was waiting for her.

'The captain has invited Marsh Faraday and his "lady" to dine with him this evening. Ever since he saw you with me the other day, it's been firmly fixed in his mind that you're my "lady". So come on, dream lover,' he tugged at her wrist, 'follow me.'

'Don't call me that,' she hissed. 'It's simply not true. How can a dream be reality? I may have dreamt about you——'

'Sweetheart, you did more than that.' His eyes twinkled down at her. 'You almost allowed me to go the whole——'

'Marsh,' she shook his hand which somehow had taken hold of hers, 'it's not true. I know that in my dream I nearly let you——' Shona coloured deeply as a memory which might have been dream, or could equally have been real, touched her mind like a match to a candle.

He bent down to whisper, 'You don't know what I know. But I hope it won't be long before you dream in my arms again.'

'I've achieved an ambition,' said Shona, leaning back against the rail gazing dreamily into Marsh's eyes.

'Let me guess,' Marsh said dryly. 'Dining at the Captain's table.'

Shona nodded. 'Thank you for letting me be your "lady" for the evening.'

'Thanks for playing the part,' he said. He put an arm on each side of her, letting the rail take his weight. 'You look very beautiful.' His eyes wandered over every feature, moved down to the rounded neckline, the softly moulded breasts, small waist, the curve of hips under the filmy skirt. 'Maybe I should write a letter of thanks to your fiancé for allowing me the pleasure of your company.'

She looked for mockery and found it in his eyes, but there was no indulgence mixed with it. 'Why does everyone call him "my fiancé"? On this ship I'm a free agent.

If he can form a—a relationship with another girl, I can form one with another man.'

'So that's what we've been doing? Forming a relationship. I must admit I've wondered. Acting as a kind of jealousy-inducer to arouse a negligent lover is new to me.'

'Please don't be sarcastic.'

'Don't you like the truth?'

Quickly she turned to lean on her arms against the rail. The setting sun threw red sparkles out across the restive sea. The ship's movement was noticeable, but little more. On the far horizon made knife-sharp by the red-gold of the sky, there was an outline of another ship. Farther along, there was another, a mere speck.

Shona felt Marsh move until his body pressed against hers. His arms wrapped around her and she shivered, not with the growing chill as the golden orb sank lower, but with delight at his touch, with a stirring of longing—and an unexplained uprush of fear.

His lips brushed her ear and he murmured, 'If I had my binoculars with me, I could tell you everything about those ships you wanted to know.' She nodded, too much under his spell to speak. 'If I had binoculars,' he went on, the movement of his lips over her throat making her cry out inside, 'I could see right into your mind.'

'And,' she whispered, 'into my heart?'

His arms around her gripped until she could hardly bear it. 'Let your heart be, Shona.' The hardness had crept into his voice. 'Don't let it become involved. It belongs to the man you're going to marry.'

She tried to escape from his imprisoning arms, but he easily held her still. 'You broke off two engagements,' she burst out, her voice as unsteady as her legs had grown. 'Why can't I break off one?'

He turned her roughly. 'Our motives have become confused. Let's sort things out.' He was becoming a stranger and she was afraid. 'Fool that I was, I agreed to this "arrangement"—to help you, please note. To bring back your straying husband-to-be.'

'But, Marsh, it hasn't had that effect, has it?' There was a plaintive note in her voice which had been put there by his attitude. Too late she realised he had interpreted it as dismay at Calvin's refusal to come to heel.

'You want to carry on this charade?' She nodded, her eyes holding his in the half-light. 'Until it's achieved its objective? Then you, my sweet,' he took her by the shoulders and walked her along the deck, 'must take the consequences, all of them, no matter what they are.'

CHAPTER EIGHT

THE audience was waiting, a blur of smiling, expectant faces under the glowing, floor-standing lamps. Emotions were ready and willing to be urged this way, persuaded that way—hers to manipulate as she pleased. Inside she was afraid—of the power laid at her feet, of the possibility of failing these people.

Outwardly she was composed, showing a calm which was a mere veneer laid there by the professionalism she had, during her training, absorbed into her system.

Toni Hardy had introduced her. Her tone had been part apologetic—after all, the star of the evening was missing and all they could offer in his place was second best—part a plea for forgiveness of the lone performer's inexperience.

To Shona, who was keyed to a state of high tension, it was magnanimous and impudent. It had the effect, not of undermining her self-confidence, but of challenging her. She would show them, she thought, all of them, everyone who doubted her ability to carry the performance on her own slender shoulders—Toni, Calvin, especially Calvin.

She heard herself saying, 'I'm here this evening to amuse you, entertain you, make you happy and sometimes make you sad. I'll play whatever you ask me to play, so think deeply, remember your old favourites, music that has meant something to you in the past, and in the present. But first I'll play a piece of my own choice. It's short and one of the best known pieces written by Litolff. It's the Scherzo from his *Concerto Symphonique*, which I've arranged as a piano solo.'

The audience, many of whom were seated in deep arm-chairs with drinks in front of them, enjoyed the music as much as Shona enjoyed playing it. It was light and happy and, she hoped, set the tone for the evening. As the applause died down and she bowed deeply, her eyes caught those of Marsh Faraday. He sat with his mother in a group of other passengers and an officer or two. His eyes were slightly mocking, his lounging figure spelling out the words, 'Entertain me—if you can.'

Shona's gaze shifted from him and she recaptured the smile which had momentarily eluded her. 'Miss Carroll,' her faithful follower, the grey-haired woman passenger, was speaking. As usual she sat as near as she could to the piano. 'I'd be so happy if you could play the Valse in E flat by Chopin.'

Shona indicated that she would be delighted to do so and announced it to the audience, who seemed to be growing in number by the minute. The notes of the familiar melody flowed from her fingers and there was a silence so deep she could hear the music echoing in her mind—which, as a musician, she knew was how it should be. When it was over there was a request from another passenger for Rubinstein's Melody in F. This, also, Shona played, delighting her listeners.

Other requests followed, including one of Tchaikovsky's *Songs Without Words* and *Clair de Lune* by Debussy. 'I shall end,' Shona told them, 'with a particular favourite of mine. It's really an orchestral theme from the ballet *Spartacus* by Khachaturian, but I've taken the main theme—it's been used as an introduction to the film series *The Onedin Line*'—there were sighs of pleasure from many people—'and adapted it for the piano.'

Shona played, losing herself in the sounds her fingers and brain were producing. The heart-lifting melody closed people's eyes and, as the climax came, moved them almost to tears. When the final notes had died away, there was a deep silence. She had taken them to the heights and they did not want to descend. Then the applause broke out.

Some of the audience stood, others stamped their feet calling 'More!' The tears in Shona's eyes as she bowed right and left in acknowledgement were not only of gratitude at their response. They were in exultation at successfully overcoming her fears and fulfilling her dream of hearing thunderous applause in appreciation of her achievements as a musician in her own right.

As she gathered the small amount of music she had brought with her, Toni Hardy emerged from the shadows. It was, she said into the microphone, the end of the concert.

'I'd like to thank the performer, Miss Carroll, for stepping in so nobly and providing us with such a happy, music-filled forty-five minutes, in spite of the fact that the real star of the evening was unable to appear. I think,' Toni turned to Shona, and there was grudging admiration in her eyes, 'it now seems that we have another star arising in the *Sea Wanderer*'s sky.'

The applause was renewed and Shona, pink now with an inner happiness which had overcome her usual deeply-embedded modesty, bowed again, including Toni this time. She caught the eye of Joe, the electrician, and found that he, too, was gazing at her with admiration. 'Great,' he whispered, 'but then I knew you had it in you.' How? she wanted to ask, but he had slipped away.

Verity Faraday waved as Shona approached. 'There's room for you next to Marsh,' she called. 'Come and have a farewell drink.'

Shona's heart bumped, then hammered on. Marsh leaving the ship? He stood up as the ship rolled a little. In a daze, Shona went with it. As Marsh's hand came out to steady her, she caught sight of an odd-looking figure lurking near the exit doors.

He wore dark glasses, roll-necked sweater and his jacket collar was turned up. Why was Calvin dressed in such a manner as to draw attention to himself, when it was obvious that that was the last thing he wanted! Marsh followed her eyes. He, too, saw the strange figure and did not bother to suppress his smile. It turned cynical as Shona veered away and went to join Calvin.

'What are you doing here?' she asked him, genuinely puzzled.

'Listening to you, though heaven knows why I bothered.'

Shona stiffened. 'I did well, you can't deny it. You must have heard how the audience responded.'

'On a cruise they'd respond with delight to a chorus of cats mewing. The noise you made was almost as unbearable.'

'Thanks for nothing,' she snapped, walking away with her head in the air. 'I didn't invite you to come and listen.' Take it from whence it comes, she told herself desperately. Take no notice of him. Surely you didn't expect praise?

He was joining her in the lift. She tried to ignore him, but the maddening need to justify herself to him conquered. 'I had to give a performance. It may not have been brilliant, but it pleased them, and that's what matters, isn't it?'

Her belief in herself was weakening already! Her carefully nurtured musical self-confidence had been growing by the second, ever since the final rapturous applause had died away. Then Calvin had come with his giant shears of sneering criticism and cut it down. And there it was, wilting and dying before her very eyes.

They were walking to their cabins. At the door of hers, Shona turned. 'All right, you've won. You've convinced me. I guess I'm still an amateur pretending to be a professional.'

'You're right,' was Calvin's spiteful answer as he took off his jacket and pulled the stifling sweater over his head. 'Don't keep fooling yourself you're my equal, Shona. Musically you never will be.'

She slammed the door on him and on what was probably the truth, she told herself miserably. Yet she had been convinced she had surpassed her usual self-negating standards and achieved new heights of performance. For a long time she stood at the window looking out at the reflected lights switchbacking over the night-darkened waves.

Marsh was going out of her life. After breakfast-time tomorrow she would never see him again. He would be disembarking at Gibraltar. No wonder he had become so thoughtful when she had mentioned the place to him. Why hadn't he told her then? Had he expected a scene—one he could not tolerate from the woman he had befriended, if that was how their very close relationship could be described?

What was a 'close relationship' to him? He had become engaged to—and left—two women. If he could play around with the affections of two other women, why should a third leave him anything but cold?

Her reflection revealed a pale, disillusioned face which only half an hour before had been lit with the inner joy of achievement and pleasure—at the giving of pleasure. A surge of misery brought with it defiance. In her wardrobe was an evening gown with a neckline which plunged deep enough to tantalise a roaming male eye. In her present mood she did not care that in design it was quite out of line with the other, more demure dresses she had brought with her for her professional appearances with Calvin.

The gown was a deep green velvet, with narrow shoulder straps which led to a point to which no other dress of hers had plunged. The back of the dress began at the waist and flared to form a tiered ankle-length skirt. If she was going to be miserable, she decided, she would at least endure that misery in style.

As she sat in the blue-tinted light of the room they called the Ocean Vista Club, occupying half of a two-seater couch in the darkest corner she could find, the defiance which had carried her there evaporated. The drink in her hand failed to stimulate. The mood music from the four-piece band only deepened her unhappiness.

She leaned back, turning her head from the dancers, the laughing, attractive women passengers and their attentive partners. Closing her eyes on the tears which nevertheless spilled over, she thought of the days, months, years to come all with one factor in common—the great emptiness which Marsh Faraday's departure from her life would create.

Mingling with her wretchedness was the terrible sense of failure which Calvin's searing criticism of her performance had implanted. He was not a man to allow personal connections to influence his musical judgments, so even in loving her—as she assumed that, in his own peculiar way, he did—he would look with impartial eyes at her piano playing. He would tell her the truth, however much it hurt. And, coming from a musician as gifted as he was, it did hurt.

Her hand was lifted and as her head swung back towards the room, a glass was put firmly into her clasp. 'Drink,' a familiar voice commanded, 'then dry those tears.'

Her trembling lips fastened on to the rim of the glass and she drank. A handkerchief was pushed into her hand and she dabbed at her eyes and her cheeks. 'Sorry,' she murmured, 'and thanks.' Her voice was tight with tension, but she hoped he would not notice.

'Now,' Marsh leaned back, arms folded, 'tell your make-believe lover all about it. If you must cry, use my shoulder.' She looked at the shoulder and found it broad and inviting. Her hand crept up to touch it. Tomorrow he would be gone. What did a small familiarity matter? He looked with amusement at her action. 'Many women have found it a convenient resting place, so there's no need to test its strength.'

Shona snatched her hand away, then reproached herself for her foolishness in thinking, even for a moment, that she meant more to this man than any of those "many women". She was silent, taking a drink and feeling it act inside her like liquid fire.

'Why didn't you accept my mother's invitation to join us after the concert?' he added.

'Oh, dear,' Shona answered, 'I didn't mean to hurt her feelings. Was she——?'

His answering smile was touched with cynicism. 'She understood when she saw who it was you were running to. Why did you go to him,' his tone had sharpened, 'as if you were on a lead and he was tugging it?'

'I—I just wondered why he was there.'

'Be honest and admit that until you'd heard the appre-ciation and praise given to you by the audience put into words by your puppet-master Calvin Faber, you wouldn't believe it yourself?'

'Puppet-master?' She flung his description back. 'He doesn't exercise any control over me.' Even as she spoke, she acknowledged that she was not being truthful. Every criticism Calvin made or—rarely—word of praise he uttered either plunged her to the depths or raised her to a plateau of pleasure.

The band played an old song, romantic, sweet. Couples danced as if no one else existed but themselves. 'He tore my performance to pieces,' Shona said flatly.

Marsh leaned forward, hands round his glass. 'You know something, Miss Carroll? He's jealous.'

Her head spun round. 'Calvin, *jealous*—of *me*? Why, he's the most fabulous up-and-coming flute player——'

Marsh held up a bored hand.

'Your praise of your loved one is becoming tedious. For heaven's sake, girl, there's such a thing as professional jealousy, isn't there?'

'Amongst players of the same instruments, maybe, but not——'

His glass hit the table with a thump. 'I can see I'm wasting my time. You refuse to see a single flaw in that gem of a man you seem to worship.' He caught her wrist and pulled her up beside him.

'I—worship Calvin? Marsh, believe me, I don't.'

They were on the dance floor, slow-dancing, cheek against cheek, his hand outspread over the bareness of her back. She felt through her dress the sensual movements of his thighs, his hard hips arousing her, the disturbing friction of his legs against hers. She knew he was dancing this way to excite her into the kind of response Calvin seemed unable and totally disinclined to do.

Her mind whispered the words, Marsh leaves tomorrow, I'll never see him again. What does it matter if I react like a real woman to his sophisticated lovemaking? When his hand slipped lower to rest possessively, then moved to her hip, she made no protest. When he lifted his cheek from hers he stared into her eyes as if testing the temperature of her feelings, she hid nothing from him.

It was all there for him to see—her pleasure in his touch, her sensuality being aroused by his, her willingness to give whatever he asked. Even the love she felt for him was written large like sky-writing against a cloudless background.

He pulled her close again and whispered above her head, 'I see all the symptoms—holiday romance, a dreading of the parting, imagined love, the "ships that pass in the night" syndrome.' She was vigorously shaking her head. 'But most of all, revenge.' Her head was still. He looked down at her. 'Ah, by elimination, the last applies.'

'No, Marsh, no.' Her cheek found his shoulder and he laughed. 'I knew you'd make use of it before the evening was out.'

The music stopped and he made to lead her from the floor. 'I'm tired, Marsh.'

He changed direction and they left the dancers and the music behind. Outside her cabin, Marsh took her key and used it. The door swung wide and he followed her in, switching on the light. 'Like any escort worth his salt, I demand a goodnight kiss.'

Her gaze was intense as she found his eyes. 'Don't you mean "goodbye"?'

He frowned. 'Who's going?' He gave her no chance to reply. She was in his arms and his lips were back in possession. Her arms lifted to cross at his neck. His whole body felt so familiar that it was almost as if they were one. Yet she was crying inside because tomorrow part of her would be torn away, never to be reunited.

A cabin door nearby opened and there was a noise outside. Slowly Marsh lifted his head and turned. Over his shoulder Shona saw that Calvin stood watching them. His hair was awry, his eyes wild. He stared at Marsh. 'You want a punch on the nose?'

Marsh drew away from Shona. 'Be careful, Mr Faber, who you challenge. I could return the compliment—in deeds, not words. Then you'd have another injury to get over.'

'Why, you——'

'The girl's all yours, Mr Faber,' Marsh drawled, pushing Shona towards him. 'She never was mine.'

As the ship made its way through the Straits of Gibraltar, the sun beat down on to Shona's shoulders and arms left bare by the strapless sundress she wore. Her arms glistened with the suntan oil she had applied and she hoped it was protecting her from the sun's hottest rays.

Through the hazy golden heat mist, rocks loomed above the ship. On one side was the faint, distant outline of the mountains and hills of Morocco. On the other was the coast of Spain.

'Last port of call before heading for home.' Marsh spoke from behind her and his two hands fastened on the ship's wide wooden rail, imprisoning her. The dark hairs on his arms did not hide his deep tan. The gold watch he wore glistened in the sun. Shona wanted to move so that her cheek rubbed against the arms. She wanted those arms to wrap about her as they had in the past.

Yet she drew herself in as if his closeness was distasteful. He had not appeared for breakfast that morning. In fact, it had been just herself and Calvin, who had taken courage from the fact that his mouth wound was now scarcely noticeable. The doctor had tentatively given the following evening as the earliest time on which he could perform again with his flute.

Marsh, it seemed, intended carrying on as if he were staying on board and not stepping off at Gibraltar and waving the ship *bon voyage*.

'Have you enjoyed the cruise?' he asked, close to her ear.

'Present tense,' she answered, feeling prickles over her skin from the caress of his breath. 'I am enjoying the cruise. It carries on for me after today,' she reminded him.

Even though, she wanted to say, I'll be dead inside with you gone.

'Happy, now your beloved has returned to your side?'

On such a beautiful day, his sarcasm grated. She would not contribute to its ruin by quarrelling, so she stayed silent. She would not tell him that as soon as he had left her last night, Calvin had returned to his cabin without speaking another word.

Her eyes wandered, tearing themselves from the endless blue sky and the hazy rocky coastline as they progressed along the Straits. Her gaze fastened again on those tanned arms.

'Go on,' Marsh's voice urged softly, 'do what you want to do. Live a little, my sweet. Let yourself go.'

Her head turned and her eyes were enmeshed with his. What was she seeking? she asked herself. Sorrow at the approaching parting, a message of everlasting love? There was mockery there, instead, and a challenge. Why should she not take up that challenge? She bent down and rested a cheek against the soft, springing hair, rubbing against the hard muscles which ran from elbow to wrist. Her lips crept round until they touched his sunburnt flesh and a quick-silver flash of longing ran through her body.

'Shona!' It was a command and she turned swiftly. His hands gripped her upper arms and he pulled her to him. His mouth captured hers and punished it with a kiss which had her teeth drawing blood inside her gums. Her lips parted at last and he must have tasted salt. How better to let him know that she would sacrifice everything, even her life's blood, for him?

'Shona?' The male voice was questioning, hesitant, then followed by a deeply apologetic, 'Sorry. Later will do.'

But Shona tore away, calling over her shoulder, 'Danny, tell me now.' With an appealing look at Marsh, she whispered, 'This is madness. Please let me go. If it's the end,' her shoulders lifted, 'it's the end, isn't it? I appreciate all you've done——'

His eyes narrowed and she was free of his hold. 'When

you marry him, I hope your life together will be happy.' He turned and walked away.

He had misunderstood! She had meant to say goodbye, but the words had come out wrongly.

'Danny,' she ran after him, 'you wanted me. What about?'

Danny looked back and saw Marsh's retreating figure. 'I didn't mean to break anything up, but I thought it was you and Calvin, not you and——'

'Forget it, Danny.' They progressed round the deck, walking against the strong breeze which played with Shona's hair.

'About this evening,' Danny said. 'The entertainments manager's asked me if you, plus me, could put on something like we did last time. Piano, guitar, and maybe me singing now and then. It would be mainly piano, of course.'

'Why should it be? You're a great performer, Danny——'

'And so are you. Isn't it time you realised? I'm just a guitar-playing guy. I don't even call myself a musician, but even I can tell that the sounds you make sure are the best sounds I've heard in a long time.'

Shona clasped his arm and gazed laughingly up at him. 'What's the ulterior motive, Danny? There's so much flattery coming from this "guitar-playing guy", there's just got to be a reason!'

'Honestly,' Danny exploded, 'you're so suspicious you even suspect a man's motives when he hands out praise. How dense can you get?'

'Please excuse me,' an icy voice requested. They moved to one side and a man overtook them. The voice and the tall, dark-haired figure were so familiar a shock ran through Shona's body. Marsh must have changed his mind and his direction and followed them. His coldness and aloof bearing wanted her to run after him and say, 'How dense can *you* get? Now that you're going, do you think I'm playing around with someone else to help get Calvin back?'

Then she thought, how *stupid* can I get? After today, I'll never see Marsh Faraday again ...

A buffet lunch was served informally on the Games Deck. People stood patiently in line waiting their turn to be given plates and cutlery. Spread out on long tables were cold meats and salads, pieces of chicken, raw, grated vegetables, cold dishes of fish of many varieties and, farther along, there were hot foods for those who fancied them.

Choice of the second course proved as difficult as the first. Apart from gateaux and sherry trifles, meringues, ice creams and fruit pies, there were biscuits and cheeses of the world and fresh fruit. These were followed by hot or cold drinks. People held plates laden with food and sought for empty seats, even finding their way to other rooms in which tables and chairs had been placed.

There was a festival atmosphere and passengers who had never met before met now and mingled and exchanged opinions and gossip and told of the different parts of the world they came from. Over the heads of other passengers, Shona saw those of Marsh and his mother. Beside Verity was the ever faithful escort, John Victor. Shona wondered idly if Marsh's mother was leaving the ship with her son. There was no doubt about it—she would miss them both.

Danny, who sat with Shona, discussed the pieces they might play that evening. He told her he knew two or three more serious works, but was an amateur in performing them. 'Ah, well,' he added ruefully, 'even if you notice my mistakes and lack of tone or whatever, the audience are so willing to be pleased, they won't.'

Which, Shona thought miserably, was almost a repeat of the words Calvin had used in describing the reception the listeners had given to her efforts on the piano. Was Calvin right, after all?

People were crowding the decks as the ship drifted slowly before the great Rock of Gibraltar. White buildings which resembled apartment blocks with four or five storeys climbed the flanks of the rock, one building upon the other, as if each block were fighting to keep its place upon the steep slope.

The quay was man-made and a two-mile drive was necessary to reach the mainland. As Shona waited in the long line for the taxis to start picking up groups of passengers and take them on a tour of the Rock, she lost Calvin, Danny and Toni. Their voices told her that they were behind her, so if she got a taxi first, she would call to them.

A taxi drew alongside, but there were others in front of her, and she made no effort to get into it. A man got out, caught her hand and tugged her into the back seat of the taxi, telling the driver to continue. She stared breathlessly at Marsh's hard profile. 'How could you?' she said. 'It wasn't my turn. And anyway, I was with——'

'You were alone,' was his crisp reply, 'and this is not an ordinary cab. It was hired especially for me. I've already been into the main street and returned—in this cab. It wasn't intended for public use.'

'But why——?' Why, since you're leaving, are you bothering about me? The words were there, clamouring to be spoken, but they remained unsaid. Instead, she said, 'Thanks, thanks a lot.'

'A mere nothing,' he said, distantly but with cynicism, 'after all the other things I've done for you since that crazy midnight promise I made at the start of the cruise.'

'If the keeping of it was all that bad,' she hit back, 'you needn't have bothered. If you'd told me how you felt, I'd never have kept you to it.'

'It was no trouble,' his eyes skimmed her bare shoulders and lingered on her throat, 'no trouble at all.'

Shona suppressed the impulse to hit back with his own brand of sarcasm. 'Where are we going?' she asked instead.

'To see the sights. In effect, you're on British soil.' And as if to prove his statement, they passed a policeman who wore a familiar British helmet. At the sight, Shona experienced a small wave of homesickness. But who, she asked herself, would want to be anywhere but where she was at that moment? In a foreign—yet not entirely foreign

—country, with the man she loved beside her, his departure from the ship—and her life—having obviously been delayed for an hour or two?

In the Main Street, people shopped and strolled. Many of them seemed of Spanish origin. There were a handful of Moorish women dressed in black from head to foot and wearing a black veil.

The drive took them across the runway of the airport. The road climbed and a long way below, the ship was a great splash of white against the deep blue of the Mediterranean Sea. Green shrubs and trees clung to the rock side and brightly-coloured flowers stood out in contrast to the rock's greyness.

Marsh pointed to a giant piece of concrete sloping steeply down the hillside. 'Water catchment area,' he explained. 'The reservoirs are cut out of solid rock. They're nearly four hundred feet above sea level.'

The cab driver enlarged, 'We are proud of our method of conserving water. The rainwater runs down the concrete surface and is carried down into ducts through a tunnel half a mile long.'

'Which,' Marsh finished, 'is where the reservoirs receive and store it. Impressed?'

'Very much indeed,' Shona answered, admiring their ingenuity.

Climbing still higher, they reached a small, wooden building made partly of logs. 'The entrance to St Michael's Cave,' said Marsh, as the driver parked in the almost empty car park. 'It's an experience not to be missed.'

As Shona got out of the taxi, she asked, 'Where are all the others?'

'They'll be here soon. We haven't stopped at any viewpoints, as they will have done, which means we've arrived here earlier.'

The interior of the cave was breathtaking. 'It's a natural limestone cavern,' Marsh told her as she gazed with unbelieving eyes at the enormous beauty of the place. 'It's used for concerts, ballet and Son et Lumière.'

There were rows of seats where the audience would no

doubt sit, terraced as the floor sloped downwards. The cavern was floodlit in brilliant colours—red, blue, green and white lights shining upon the magnificent stalagmites and stalactites, adding an awesome drama to the natural formations which had come into being over millions of years.

The stone steps which took the visitor downwards were not illuminated and Shona faltered, looking for support as she went down each one. Once she missed and found herself groping for the ground, hitting it with her hand and grazing a knee slightly as she stumbled.

Strong hands came out to help her up. Marsh shook his head, tutting. 'I leave her for a few seconds and she overbalances. What will you do when I've gone out of your life for good?' He was smiling, but she wanted to cry out, until her voice echoed down the aeons of time in which this cavern was formed, Never leave me, never go away!

He took out a handkerchief and in the cavern's dimness wiped her hand which had come away from the rocky surface wet and dirty. Her knee, too, although only slightly hurt, was damp. He crouched to dab at it with yet another clean handkerchief and she shivered. Not only was the air cool after the hot sun outside, Marsh's touch made her tremble.

'All right now?' he asked, and she nodded. 'Stay close,' he ordered, and put an arm across her shoulders. 'Each step I take, you take, too. As if,' he added, and his eyes glowed red, blue and green, mesmerising her, 'we were one.'

Was the magic of the place getting into him, as well as into her? Slowly they descended, down, down again, gazing high at the roof which disappeared into darkness, listening to the music and the singing voices which came at them from all sides as someone switched on a tape.

Above there were row upon row of giant stalactites, like massive canine teeth. In many places stalactites reached down and met stalagmites pushing upwards sometimes to form giant pillars, narrow in the centre and broadening above and below. Shona saw with strange fascination some stone steps which in turn led to nowhere but a black, un-lighted well disappearing below into more darkness. A barrier had been placed in position, cutting off the unknown dangers.

Marsh strolled down another pathway into deep shadow. There he pulled her round to face him. She gazed up, knowing he was there but seeing not even a shadow, nor an outline. A mouth claimed hers and she clasped her arms round the man, urging against him, escaping into him, trying to show him the depth of her love. The music came from every corner and alcove. Magic and mystery lurked everywhere, penetrating the mind and the body, all mixing and merging into one throbbing, momentous kiss.

Climbing up the steep slope of the gangway, Shona showed her landing card while Marsh received a brief salute.

'I must find my mother and collect the luggage. The taxi will be here soon.'

This was goodbye and he was in such a hurry he had no time to spare to say that word? Had her entry into his life, and now departure, made so little impression he could go, just like that, snapping his fingers, almost, in her face?

'Thank you for the tour of the Rock,' she managed to say without choking with tears.

He smiled. 'I enjoyed every moment, Miss Carroll, even though I've seen it many times before. I saw it with different eyes,' his fingers pressed against each cheek bone beneath her eyes, 'yours. I enjoyed the sunshine and the shadows, particularly,' his smile grew slightly mocking, 'the shadows.'

He was gone, moving up the stairs two at a time. He did not even turn for a final look. Moodily, Shona gazed in the windows of the Tropics Shop. It was closed, as were the other shops while in port. Later, when they were under way again, they would re-open. On display was a tee-shirt in white, with scarlet letters saying, 'Come to sea with O.R.C.' Ocean Rover Cruises, Shona interpreted. Maybe she would buy one ...

Listlessly she turned away and bumped into Danny. 'Got you,' he said, linking her arm in his. 'Let's rehearse.'

'Usual place?' Danny nodded, and Shona, going up the stairs at his side, asked, 'Where's Toni, Danny?'

'With Calvin in the Ocean Vista Club annexe. He's trying to get his lips to his flute again. Judging by the choice words coming from the room as I went past, he wasn't doing so well. Here we are. Here's some music I grabbed from my cabin. Lighter than your usual stuff, but there's one or two more difficult pieces I'll try out. If you can't stand the noise, tell me and I'll stop.'

'No, you won't stop, Danny. You'll keep right on until you get it right. I'm not a music teacher for nothing.'

He caught her smile. 'You, a music teacher? I thought you were a concert pianist.' Shona pointed to herself and shook her head unbelievingly. 'Honestly, you're good enough to be.'

They sorted through the music scores and the rehearsal began.

Dressing early for dinner, Shona stood at her cabin window looking at the towering Rock that was Gibraltar. She remembered its rugged steepness, the view across the Straits to the mist-shrouded land of Morocco, the blueness of the sky which was reflected in the Mediterranean Sea. Most of all she could not forget St Michael's Cave, the awe-inspiring beauty of wild nature partially tamed, the echoing beauty of the music—and the abandoned, desperate farewell kiss between herself and Marsh.

Her disconsolate mind added weight to her limbs and swept the holiday eagerness from her eyes. As she walked down the stairs to the Equator Room to read until dinner, she passed the deck to which the gangway had been fixed for exit and entrance to the ship.

About to turn the corner to descend yet another staircase taking her to the deck she wanted, there were voices at the entrance, a sound of people arriving at the top of the gangway and requesting help with their luggage.

Shona stopped incuriously to watch the new passengers' arrival. When Marsh stepped on board, Shona's heart nearly stopped. Abandoning all restraint, she cried out his name and closed the gap between them, flinging her arms round his neck.

He gazed down at her, as if puzzled by her action. He held hand luggage and his arms stayed weighted down at his sides. Shona was left clinging to him and saying, tears of happiness clouding her eyes, 'I thought you'd gone. You said you were disembarking.'

He frowned. 'It was my mother who left the ship, with John Victor. They're staying a few days and then flying home. She asked me to say goodbye and was sorry she missed you.' He had spoken quietly, completely devoid of emotion.

Even as she released him, sensing that something was wrong, she glimpsed over his shoulder a tall blonde-haired woman. 'But your mother's behind you——' she blinked away the tears and saw that the blonde she had seen was, if anything, younger than Marsh, and only a few years older than herself. Anyone less 'motherly' was hard to conceive.

'I'm sorry,' Shona backed away. 'Regard my—my welcome as coming from a—a rather naïve child.' The bitterness was there for everyone to hear—and interpret as they wished. She had presumed upon the former intimacies, their passionate kisses, imbuing them with a meaning they plainly did not possess.

The blonde smiled. 'Another conquest, Marsh?'

He performed the introduction, ignored the question. 'Marguerite, meet Shona, Shona Carroll, a member of our entertainments crew. Shona, Marguerite Blandish.' Shona was left in ignorance as to the blonde's identity, knowing only, by an encompassing, if prejudiced glance, that she was his mother's height—which had been only a few inches shorter than himself—that her hair was as elegantly styled as Verity's had been but that she was a far less likeable person.

The newcomer's hand came out. 'Marsh, darling,' Shona

put her hand in the woman's and quickly retrieved it, 'you forgot to mention who I am.'

'Model?' Shona intervened quickly.

'Excellent guess, Miss Carroll. Ocean River Cruises are bringing out a new brochure and use people like me to decorate their photographs.'

Shona frowned. 'But we're on our way home. All the blue skies are behind us.'

'This young lady friend of yours, Marsh, is so perspicacious.' The drawled sarcasm aroused Shona's anger, but Marsh's goading smile revealed how he was enjoying the feline exchange. 'The next cruise is to the Mediterranean, so it's those blue skies which will be the background. You see, I shall stay on the ship. Darling,' to Marsh, 'take pity on your fiancée and lead me to my cabin. I hope it's not too far from yours.'

'It's on a lower deck,' he said briskly, retrieving the hand baggage, then calling for a bellboy to take his companion's cases.

'Which fiancée would you be, Miss Blandish?' Shona asked sweetly. 'Number one or two? I hear Marsh is an expert at ditching women he gets tired of.'

'Marsh!' Her scandalised frown told him to put this upstart member of the entertainments crew in her place.

'For all you know, Miss Carroll,' he said softly, 'she's number three.' And he led the way to the new arrival's cabin.

So Marsh was back on board, but for all the joy she was going to get out of it, he might have stayed in Gibraltar with his mother.

Dinner would have been a painful affair conversationally if there had not been two new faces at their table. It was, at first, with anger that Shona saw as she approached her usual place that Marsh had decided to desert in his mother's absence, and find fresh seating.

When, with Calvin, she settled at the table and in the shy silence that often precedes the making of a new acquaintance, Shona considered Marsh's defection, she decided that it was for the best. Since the woman who called herself his fiancée was so different in personality from his very pleasant mother, and since there already seemed to be an antipathy between herself and Marsh's new companion, dinner might have been distinctly uncomfortable.

The couple who sat with them now were middle-aged and had, they said, spent ten days in Gibraltar. 'Did you know,' the woman, who introduced herself as Joyce Marten, said, 'that there aren't any cows on the Rock?'

'For obvious reasons,' said her husband Reginald. 'They'd fall off!'

'And,' his wife went on, 'they have to import all their milk? And nearly all their food.'

'Meat, vegetables, fruit. The Rock's three miles long and fourteen hundred feet high.'

'We saw the apes,' Joyce Marten continued. 'Did you know they're really a tailless kind of monkey? They came from Morocco and Gib's the only place in Europe where you can find them. The Military look after them, and very careful they are with them, too. But they warn you not to get too close to the apes, or they might make off with your handbag or camera!'

Mentally staggering under the weight of information which had suddenly been unloaded on to them, Shona smiled and showed the interest she felt. Having been so preoccupied with the presence of the man whose taxi she was sharing, she had missed such pieces of information. Calvin showed unusual interest, too, and came out of his slightly surly silence to carry on a conversation. His lip had healed, leaving only a slight scar which would go with time.

Shona searched for Marsh, seeing the expertly coiffured head of his companion first. It was, as she had guessed, at the Captain's table that they sat. How would the gentlemanly and gracious Captain accept the woman called Marguerite as Marsh Faraday's newly-acquired 'lady'? In view of Marsh's important position in the shipping company, without a flicker of his eyelid probably!

As Calvin walked to the lift at Shona's side, he said, 'Where's this evening's brilliant performance going to take place?'

'I can only do my best, Calvin,' Shona said quietly.

'Which,' said Calvin expansively as they waited for the lift, 'considering you only came on board as my accompanist, isn't that bad, I suppose. But with this untutored audience,' he looked disdainfully around, 'you could get away with musical murder and it wouldn't be noticed.'

He looked over his shoulder again, then stared at the carpet beneath his feet. A crowd had gathered to await the lift's arrival, and as Shona followed the path Calvin's eyes had taken she saw just behind them the tall, lazily smiling figure of Marsh Faraday. At his side, with her arm linked through his, was his fiancée.

Turning back to lift-watching, Shona said, 'The concert's in the Orchid Room. Danny and I have put a programme together. It should please most tastes. Except yours,' she added acidly, as the lift arrived at last.

'True,' Calvin answered, completely serious. He made for the back of the lift. 'The only music on the ship that pleases me is what I produce on my flute.'

Aghast at this public display of his enormous conceit, Shona stared at him, seeking humour in his face, but there was nothing there. The only amusement she found was in the curved lips and hooded eyes of the man to whom she had so completely and so catastrophically given her heart. And he, it appeared, had all the time been engaged to be married . . .

CHAPTER NINE

THE Orchid Room was full to capacity. The grey-haired lady was, as usual, at the front. Marsh was seated to one side with his lady companion beside him. She was smoking, tapping her cigarette at intervals and with studied grace into a floor-standing metal ashtray at her side. On her face was an expression of exaggerated boredom.

That evening the music ran, with the purity of a crystal-clear stream, from Shona's fingers. She played a piano arrangement of the old English song *Greensleeves*, which delighted the audience, and followed this with a Chopin Nocturne. Then she played a piano arrangement of the song *Softly Awakes My Heart*, with Danny accompanying her on his guitar. They were bowing, intending to announce that they would play two or three requests before bringing the concerto to a close, when someone called from the audience, 'How about a repeat of the *Sea Wanderer* Concerto?'

Shona and Danny looked at each other. 'Could we?' Shona asked Danny quietly.

'I'll have a darned good try,' he answered. 'It's still all in here. How about you?'

'Every note,' Shona replied, and turned back to the audience, telling them that by special request they would play ... The rest was drowned in applause.

Shona caught a glimpse of Calvin standing in a slightly belligerent fashion at the back of the large room. It was as if he couldn't bring himself to venture another step nearer to the source of the music. At the request for the concerto, he had grimaced and with a dismissing movement of his head, dissociated himself from the rest of the audience.

His attitude incensed Shona and she sat, spreading the skirt of her long dress and attempting to prepare herself

163

mentally to play. Another glance round brought her eyes up against those of Marsh Faraday. A small smile played about his lips. There was challenge, too, but it did not say, 'You'll flounder, sure as I'm standing here,' as Calvin's did. It said, 'If you've got any ability at all, I dare you to prove it.'

I'll prove it, she thought, I'll prove it all right! And, with Danny's skilled accompaniment, she did. The applause seemed to make the ship pitch and toss even though they had not long left Gibraltar behind. It was as though she alone was on a storm-harassed sea and the audience around her becalmed. For a moment she thought she was going to faint and sent an involuntary distress message to Marsh.

As she bowed and bowed again, holding Danny's hand, the faintness passed and she emerged into a world of pleasure, congratulation and relief. An arm went round her waist. A deep, familiar voice to which she had no right to respond so warmly—he belonged to another woman as she herself was supposed to belong to another man—asked if she was in need of a drink.

Thanking him distantly for his thought—if she had responded as she wanted she would have been in his arms—she went to turn away, but Marsh said, 'You did well. You've left your mark on this ship and this particular set of passengers as no other performer has done. They'll never forget the magic music you created and produced for them alone—as they will regard it.'

'You're being very kind,' she answered in a professionally formal tone.

'I'm a very kindly person,' was the dry answer spoken in an entirely informal way. Then he turned to the audience.

'One word before you go, ladies and gentlemen.' Marsh's voice was raised to capture their attention. 'I'd like to tell you something that even Miss Carroll doesn't know. The first performance of her *Sea Wanderer* Concerto was recorded on to tape and the directors of Ocean Rover Cruises have decided to adopt the concerto as their own theme music. It will be played often over the public address system and also each time the ship leaves a major world port.'

There was an outburst of applause and Shona stared at Marsh, astonishment and delight lighting up her face. Cameras flashed, Danny was invited to join her and then Marsh. It was some time before the picture-taking stopped, and when it did, Marsh bowed to Shona briefly and left her.

Danny said, 'Whew, what a climax! Can I kiss the beautiful composer?' He bent to kiss her cheek. Others shook her hand and Joe the electrician said at her side, 'You didn't know the other evening, did you, that I was recording you? I knew all about it.'

'You might have told me,' she laughed.

'What, and made you self-conscious?' He lifted a hand and was gone.

Danny approached. 'I'm having a quick drink and then I'm going up to the theatre to watch the show. They're doing excerpts from *South Pacific* and *Oklahoma* and Toni's in it. Coming?'

'Maybe I'll join you later, but just now I'll unwind in my cabin. Okay?'

Danny saluted and made for the nearest bar. Shona looked for Calvin, but he had gone. As she walked through the long room towards the exit doors, she found herself automatically looking for Marsh. She discovered him sitting beside the woman called Marguerite. With one or two other passengers, they sat around a table on which a wine waiter was placing drinks.

Marsh looked up, catching her eyes on him. Tentatively she smiled, the sense of elation giving her the courage she would otherwise have lacked. But it was as if she was a stranger to him now that his fiancée had joined him. Someone passing said, 'That was just wonderful, Miss Carroll.'

Shona turned her back on Marsh's coolly appraising eyes and told the woman passenger that she was only too happy to have given her such pleasure. For much of the way back to her cabin, it was the same. People stopped for a word of thanks and appreciation. Throwing open her cabin door, she seized the Spanish doll, then threw herself on to her bed. Holding the doll to her cheek, she murmured, 'I've proved it to myself at last. I can play, I can really play the piano—as a pianist in my own right.'

'Don't you mean "in your own wrong"?' It was Calvin in her doorway. She sat up, putting aside the doll.

'No, I don't. I'm a fully-fledged pianist now—*and* a composer.'

His laugh was derisory and spiteful. 'Call what you did playing the piano? One of the kids you teach could have done better.'

He turned away and Shona rose, following him to his own cabin. He sat on the bed which had been turned down with care by the cabin steward.

'What's the matter, Calvin?' Shona asked in a tortured voice. 'Why are you so nasty to me about my playing? Can't you even congratulate me about the concerto? Everyone else has been so pleasant, telling me how much enjoyment I've given them——'

He picked up his flute and fingered it lovingly. 'They've given you a big head, that's obvious. This ship might be large, but it's not the whole wide world. There isn't one music critic on board, and even if there was, he'd be on holiday and have his claws sheathed.'

For a moment Shona could not speak. She was convinced to the very heart of her that she'd been good that evening. She'd given her playing everything she'd got, it had poured from her, the sounds roaring in her ears and coursing in a torrent through her hands striking the piano keys. And then the announcement Marsh had made . . .

She leaned back against the door, bracing herself against the movement of the ship, 'You're supposed to be my fiancé, Calvin, yet,' she steadied her wavering voice, 'you're so—so nasty. Every time I perform in public, no matter how hard I try, you demean my performance, tearing it to shreds and, as if that wasn't enough, stamping on it.' Her heart drummed, her eyes moistened. 'Calvin, you're killing my confidence, you're murdering my self-respect. You'll have to stop it, Calvin, or I'll——'

There was a thought inside her brain that grew and grew, and her eyes grew wider and wiser. She knew the answer and it had her gasping. 'It's true, after all! You're jealous, Calvin, jealous—of my success, of my ability and of my growing stature in the musical world.'

It was as though she'd exploded a bomb at his feet. He flung his flute on to the bed. 'Me,' he pounded his chest with his fist, '*jealous*? Of you? Of your rotten little concerto, your fumbling playing,' his voice had risen almost to a shriek, 'of your miserable technique and your—your ineptness?' His hands grasped her shoulders and they shook her. He was in a frenzy of anger and she was too stunned to do anything but stare. 'You're lousy, do you hear? You're a rotten little musician. In fact, it's desecrating the word "musician" to apply it to you ...'

He turned away and his hands went to his face, covering it. His shoulders shook and after a few seconds there was a sound of sobbing. Calvin—Calvin was crying. Calvin, the brilliant flautist, 'virtuoso' some had called him, a genius, making his instrument talk ... he was as unsure of himself and as jealous of others' successes as any other average, ordinary human being.

Enlightenment had her eyes drying and her heartbeats slowing. Compassion had pity opening up inside her like a flower as dawn lightens the sky. It was never love that had made her accept this man's proposal of marriage, but a kind of hero-worship, an infatuation not with him as a man but with him as a musical genius.

She had put him on a pedestal—which was where he had wanted to be—and now he had fallen and the image of him that she had placed high and out of her reach was lying in fragments at her feet. But she wouldn't tread on them. She wouldn't even kick them out of the way.

Softly she walked across to him, put a hand on his shoulder, which he shook off. Undaunted, her hand went back and this time he allowed it to stay. 'I think I understand now, Calvin.' She sat beside him on the bed. She took one of his hands in both of hers. Talented and distinguished in musicianship though he was, his ego and his confidence needed boosting just as much as lesser mortals, maybe even more, since his standards of achievement were so much higher.

'On the last night of the cruise,' she encouraged, 'when we play together again, *you* will be the star, Calvin, just as you've always been. After a rest, you'll play even better—if that's possible.'

A faint tinge coloured his pale cheeks. Calvin was blushing! It seemed that, as her belief in her own talent had grown, so his had lessened, taking his self-assurance with it. 'Oh, Calvin,' she put the back of his hand to her cheek, 'how could you ever stop believing in yourself? You'll reach the heights while I'm still at the foot of the mountain!'

He managed a smile and she pulled his head down to her shoulder, putting her arm across him. He had turned momentarily into a young boy, clutching at any show of affection, any words of praise that came his way. 'Calvin,' Shona murmured, 'you know we can't marry, don't you? We're more like brother and sister, really, aren't we?' He hesitated, then nodded, staying where he was.

More like mother and child, Shona thought ruefully, but did not dare to say so. 'I'm fond of you, you know,' she soothed, stroking his hair. 'We must stay friends, but I'll give you back your ring.'

'Will you keep it?' There was a hint of the familiar forcefulness and Shona did not resent it. 'It didn't cost a great deal. I'd intended buying you a better one, but there never seemed to be the time.'

'One day, when you're famous all over the world,' she humoured him, 'and your name is on everyone's lips, I'll look at it and it'll remind me of you.'

He lifted his head, smiled and put her hand to his cheek as she had done to his, then his head sank to her shoulder again. Feed his pride and he'll eat out of your hand. The words came out of nowhere and she smiled at the vanity of the man.

'Shona?' Her eyes swerved to the door. Marsh filled the entrance to the cabin. He looked from one to the other. His eyes came to rest on her wide open gaze. 'Promise fulfilled?' he asked. It was not really a question but a statement of fact. He turned and went away.

Shona closed her eyes. The end of an 'arrangement', she thought, her throat tight, and the end of a dream.

Two more days, Shona reminded herself as she dressed next morning, then back to normality and home. No more Marsh Faraday, not even a sight of his tall, commanding figure with the blonde permanently at his side.

Shona stayed in Calvin's cabin for most of the morning, listening to him practising. He asked for criticism but, knowing him better now, she gave only praise and encouragement. When she told him she wanted to visit the on-board shops, he nodded absently and she knew he would not miss her.

Wishing to buy something which would remind her of the cruise, Shona decided on a *Sea Wanderer* pen. She was fascinated by the bone china and the sets of crystal drinking glasses and ornaments. The cameras caught her eye and the pocket radios.

'Darling,' the affected voice drifted across the shop and Shona did not need to turn to know who was speaking, 'just look at these wonderful Lladro horse figures! Oh, I *wish* I'd brought my purse. Darling, could you——?'

Shona smiled as she heard Marsh's request for the item to be given to the lady and the till rang up the amount of the purchase.

'Oh, darling, thank you! Look, Madge, what Marsh has bought me. Isn't it just fabulous?'

An arm brushed against Shona's, a thigh made familiar contact with hers. Shona breathed, without looking up, 'Oh, *darling*, just look at that wonderful gold watch. Oh, if only I hadn't left my purse in my cabin!'

Her eyes lifted in sarcastic challenge. Marsh's eyes held a glint which told her he had accepted the challenge. 'You want a gold watch, Miss Carroll? You shall have one. Make your choice.'

'Don't be silly.' She was worried now and stole a glance over her shoulder at his fiancée. 'You can't give another woman a present, especially with your own woman just over there.'

'I can do what the hell I like,' he answered pleasantly. 'You threw down the challenge and spiced it with sarcasm —directed at *my woman*. I accept that challenge and throw your sarcasm back in your stupid, if beautiful, face.'

'I can do what I like, too.' She started to turn, but Marsh's arm held her back.

'You refuse to select one, so I'll choose.' He picked up the most delicate of the range and the most expensive. 'Duty-free shop,' he smiled sardonically, 'so remember to declare it at Customs, otherwise you might find your-self——' he flicked her figure with his gaze, 'in the arms of Authority. And they're not nearly so warm as mine.'

Shona shook her head. 'I can't take it, Marsh——'

'Your husband-to-be wouldn't like it? Okay,' he handed the watch over the counter and produced a wad of notes, 'call it a re-engagement present.' An eyebrow flicked up mockingly, and was coupled with a jeering smile. The watch, boxed and wrapped, was placed in his hands and he walked out of the shop. His fiancée was nowhere to be seen.

He pulled Shona to a bench seat near the shop, took the watch from its wrappings and fastened his fingers round her left wrist. Bemused, she offered no resistance. As she contemplated the watch, her throat grew thick with emotion. All she could do was shake her head again and gaze at him. The only word she could think of was, 'Why?'

'Why not? To embarrass you, maybe? You were being cheeky, you can't deny it. To thank you—you've given a lot of pleasure to a lot of passengers. To thank you again— for what you've given me.' His cynical smile robbed the words of the tenderness which might have made her reach up and kiss him.

Her lower lip pushed outward covering her top lip. When the trembling stopped she answered, 'We made that arrangement that night. Whatever I——' she took a steadying breath, 'gave you was in the form of—of thanks.'

'Just as long as our objective has been fulfilled.' There was a curious hardness in his voice. 'Has it?'

She made her expression blank. 'You saw us together last night in Calvin's cabin.'

'It was a touching scene.'

Steeling herself to his mockery, she said, 'Well, now you know the answer.'

Marsh pushed the box and wrappings into his pocket and walked away.

Shona spent the afternoon wandering round the ship. Time and again she sought for the watch and fingered it lovingly. In one shop she bought a silk headscarf and a beaded evening bag, in another, a recorded cassette of classical music. In a third shop she chose a silver necklet with a silver charm of the ship which she wore immediately. Buying other items as gifts to friends on her return, she took them to her cabin and found that Calvin's door was closed. The sound of his playing drifted out, so she resumed her wandering.

The library was filling up again with returned books, some of them adventure stories, others romantic novels, while a number were non-fiction books about other parts of the world. She stayed there for some time, then wandered around the Games Deck, watching people play deck quoits. At the tennis courts she stopped.

Two of the players stood out by the expert way they played. Marsh Faraday, Shona thought, would stand out in a milling crowd or alone on a deserted beach. His opponent, not quite his match in expertise but not far short of it, was his blonde fiancée. Marsh played a hard game and, instead of tiring as it progressed, his energies seemed to increase.

He had glanced to the side once in the course of the

game. It was as if his eyes had been drawn there by Shona's
concentration on him. It seemed to take him only seconds
to sum up her state of mind and it was not until she saw
his narrow-eyed appraisal that she realised how forlorn she
had been feeling—and therefore, she guessed, looking.

Marsh won the game, going at the end to the net to take
the hand of his opponent, in the true sportsmanlike manner, even though she happened also to be his fiancée. He
also took a kiss which she appeared only too willing and
eager to bestow on him.

In disgust, although she admitted to herself that she had
no right to be so, Shona turned away. After that, wherever
she went, Marsh and Marguerite were around somewhere.
She could hear Marsh's laughter, Marguerite's affected,
high-pitched speaking voice. Even at tea in the restaurant,
they were there at the next table, talking with immense
ease to the passengers who had joined them at the large,
round table.

It was the same that evening after dinner. Even when she
walked with Calvin around the deck with the wind blowing
enough to cause her to put on a jacket, Shona saw coming
towards them two figures with their arms wrapped around
each other.

If Marsh had not smiled, just a little too broadly to be
trusted, and Marguerite had not put on her most charming
expression and gracefully inclined her head, model-fashion,
Shona would not even have shown recognition. Calvin,
whose hands were thrust deep in his pockets, lifted his head
sufficiently to nod. Shona said a distant, 'Good evening.'
The happy, laughing couple passed by.

Anger mixed with desolation made a distasteful cocktail,
Shona discovered as she and Calvin continued their walk.
After Marsh's kisses, his lovemaking and his passion, she
wanted no other man's hands to touch her, let alone attempt
to arouse.

Yet there was Marsh cheerfully escorting—no, flaunting
for all to see would be more accurate—a woman whose
existence Shona had not even guessed at in the course of

her strange and ardent relationship with him.

That evening, Shona persuaded Calvin to accompany her to the Pool Bar.

'I can't dance,' Calvin mumbled, walking with her and clinging to the handrail along the corridor as the ship rolled now and then. 'Especially in these unstable conditions.'

'I'm not asking you to dance,' Shona said patiently. 'Just to be my partner.'

And that was precisely what Calvin proved to be in the half-light of the room where the four-piece band played and the dancers danced, fast or slow as the music dictated. Wine waiters moved around the tables and, when one approached, Calvin ordered two dry sherries.

While they drank, Calvin gazed around, his manner withdrawn. It was when Shona looked at him as the waiter approached again that she saw Calvin was reading a folded-back paperback book. How he could read the print Shona could hardly guess, except that there was a well-shaded lamp on the table. It was, of course, a book about music.

Calvin shook his head at the waiter's question, but Shona asked for a repeat of the first drink. Calvin paid automatically when it came and went on reading.

A couple entered and when Shona saw it was the man for whom she had been searching since she and Calvin had arrived, her heart did a double beat. As if a switch had been flicked inside, Marguerite began to act the irresistible model.

There was no doubting Marsh's desire to be enchanted by the girl who was now dancing clasped in his arms and urging herself as close as she dared, in the circumstances, to his body. Marguerite gazed, transfixed, into Marsh's eyes, sang with mobile lips the words to the music and with her legs managed even to insinuate herself into the movements of his limbs.

As they swung round—Marguerite managed to make even a romantic dance seem second cousin to a display of judo—Marsh looked across the room to where Shona sat with Calvin. In the few moments in which he faced them, he seemed to have assessed the situation which prevailed at the table and found it deeply amusing.

In a twisted act of defiance, Shona called the waiter and ordered yet another sherry. Calvin looked up, registering surprise, but returned at once to his reading. When the drink was placed in front of her, Calvin's hand went automatically to his pocket, but Shona forestalled him, paying the waiter herself.

Marsh led his fiancée to a table while the musicians rested. As they drank, the music started again and Marguerite was on her feet pulling at Marsh's hand.

A passenger approached Shona, her husband behind her. With a polite nod to Calvin, she said, 'I just want to thank you, Miss Carroll, for all the pleasure you've given me on this cruise.'

'Me, too,' her husband added. 'Please let me get you a drink. We can't thank you in any other way . . .'

Shona was beginning already to feel the effects of her slightly reckless drinking but felt that in the circumstances it would be uncivil to shake her head, so she thanked the man instead. 'Dry Martini?' she ventured. A few moments' chat and grateful thanks later, the order arrived. The couple left and as Shona lifted the glass to drink, Calvin asked mildly, 'Should you?'

'Why not?' Even Shona recognised her growing belligerence, but she was beyond caring. 'I'll have another if I want,' she added, conscious that her words were no longer crystal clear. The liquid slipped down her throat and the room began, very gently, to revolve.

Leaving her bag on the table beside Calvin, she stood up. She felt for the gold watch as if gaining courage from its presence. The ship, she thought, is rolling badly tonight. However, on looking round, she saw that others seemed to be walking and dancing without trouble.

'Going to get some air,' she mumbled.

Making the swing doors, not without difficulty and a few surprising stumbles, she found herself on the topmost tier around the swimming pool. Holding the handrail all the way, she reached the pool's side and gazed wonderingly into it.

There was water in the pool—she could hear it flapping and slapping against the sides as the ship moved. Blue water, she thought, only it looked black now. Sparkling, inviting water, she thought, although only a pale moon and a few stars were in the night sky and they, without the sun's power, left the water dark.

The ship rolled and Shona stiffened against it, feeling water splash over her evening sandals. Dampness made the long straight skirt of her dress cling to her ankles and she shivered, feeling the breeze playing round her bare arms and shoulders. Wishing she had brought her shawl and that the water had stayed where it belonged—in the pool—she braced herself and stepped backwards, only to feel the deck slope again under the movement of the waves.

In the time it took for the vessel to right itself, her feet had begun to slip on the wet tiles. Her arms, now flung wide, were useless in helping her keep her balance. There was nothing within reach to hold on to. As she slid helplessly towards the gaping hole that was the swimming pool, she heard herself cry out. The music drowned both her voice and the splash she made as she hit the water, face down.

Her body went under and after seconds which, to her, seemed like hours, she surfaced and gasped. In vain her hands groped for the rail. She tried floating on her back, but the water was so choppy as a result of the ship's movement and the strong breeze playing over it, she was turned on to her front.

Her hair clogged her mouth, her nose and her eyes and she could only breathe in gasps. For some reason her legs would not kick and she wished she had not had those drinks. It seemed to her in her confusion that her legs were bound by bandages then she realised that it was the tight skirt of her dress that was hampering her leg movements so that she couldn't even swim.

Panic began in her heart and spread upwards to her head, filling her brain with screaming fantasies, with devilish faces and blinding, brilliant colours. It was only when she surfaced again that she realised she had been under for the second time. There was a roaring in her ears and choking sobs racked her chest.

Through a haze there appeared the shape of a man. He was pulling off his clothes and she wondered why. There was a great splash and after a moment strong arms supported her, dragging her to the side, taking the weight of her and carrying her up and out of the angry, hungry depths.

'Marsh,' she gasped, her head trying unsuccessfully to find his shoulder and hanging back, 'put me down and leave me! Go——' her head lifted and fell again, 'go back to your—your woman!'

'You'd rather have your fiancé?' Marsh's voice was as cold as the water he had lifted her from.

She shook her head but found it too much effort. 'Not my fiancé, not any more.' Her voice sounded peculiar, thick and slurred. She was placed roughly face down on the tiles and hands were pressed cruelly hard against her back. 'No water, Marsh,' she gasped, 'didn't swallow any. Spat it out.'

The pressure eased and she lay limply, head to one side. She heard Marsh call, 'Marguerite, get Faber.'

'No, no,' Shona protested and turned on to her back. 'Want to get up, want to stand. I'm c-cold, Marsh. Warm me, please warm me.' A towel landed near her and moments later it was around her, absorbing the wet.

'Faber?' Marsh's voice echoed in the arena of the pool area. 'Your fiancée—she was in the pool. Will you take over? Get a doctor to her?'

There was a silence that seemed to last for an eternity, then Calvin said slowly, echoing the words which Marsh had only a few days before said to him.

'She's all yours, Mr Faraday. She's never been mine.'

With that he walked slowly away.

CHAPTER TEN

'So I acted too well? I over-played the part?' Marsh's voice was grating against the dull ache in her head.

Shona opened her eyes after a period of what must have been sleep. It couldn't have been unconsciousness. Surely even Marsh Faraday would have been more sympathetic if she had been affected that badly by the near-drowning she had experienced?

Her hand went to her eyes. 'What do you mean?' She moved her hand to look round. As she had guessed, she was in Marsh's Seascape Suite, and the diffused lighting was kind to her, which was more than she could say of her host!

There seemed to be the softness of a bed beneath her sagging limbs, a pillow under her still damp hair. Her dress was in a pile on the floor. Hastily she looked down at herself and the colour crept into her cheeks. Someone had stripped her down to her underwear, which was very brief indeed. Her hands lifted quickly to cover the part of her anatomy which Marsh's eyes seemed to find fascinating.

'Who——?' she asked angrily, looking round for the presence of a woman. 'Not you?'

'Who else but me? Or would you have preferred me to call the cabin steward to dry your inert but delightful body?'

Her hands stayed, a little futilely, in position. Her head turned to one side and her eyes squeezed shut. 'Please cover me.'

There was a low laugh. 'Trying to pretend it's not happening by behaving like a child? My sweet, you're no child. What shall I cover you with—myself?'

'Don't you dare, Marsh Faraday,' she choked. Her hands felt around for a bedcover, but she discovered that since she was lying on top of them, there was no way, other than sliding off the bed, and into it, of pulling them over her. Quickly her hands returned to cover herself again and Marsh laughed derisively.

'My hair's still wet. I need a towel.' Marsh did not move from where he stood beside the bed. She rolled on to her front, managing as she did to pull a cover with her.

He moved and there was a rough, rubbing motion over the back of her head. 'No,' she rolled on to her back and the cover opened out again, 'I'll dry my hair.' He let her have the towel and a few minutes later she realised why. In occupying her hands, she had left her body free for his intrigued inspection. 'Give me my clothes!' she almost shouted.

'Okay.' His acquiescence surprised her until she saw the reason. He held up her dripping evening dress. 'This? It's all there was. A dress, a gold watch and those——' he indicated her underpants, 'and then—delight of delights, nothing. Just you.'

The dress piled on to the floor. His feet brought him nearer and Shona's hand rested agitatedly on her damp head. He came to a stop at the bedside.

'You've been delivered into my hands by your husband-to-be. He must be a peculiar kind of man. In no circumstances would I give away my woman to another man. Especially,' his voice dropped, 'one as luscious as this.'

Shona pressed the draped towel closer to her. At least it constituted some barrier to his wandering eyes.

'Which,' he continued, 'is what I meant just now when I said that maybe I'd overplayed the part of the makebelieve lover. From what Faber said, he seems to think I'm in love with you.' He spoke as if the idea afforded him a great deal of amusement.

'That wasn't what he meant,' Shona snapped, angered by his heartless attitude. 'How could he when you're an engaged man yourself?'

He looked with a kind of interested detachment at her tousled hair, dwelt on her large brown eyes which were warily watching him and trying to gauge his next move. His eyes glinted, as if he were enjoying playing her on the end of a line. He sat on the bed, thumbs hooked in his belt. The bed was wide, as was its twin on the other side of the table. Wide though it was, Shona felt no urge at all—although she knew she should have done—to edge away from him.

'I saw you go out of the Pool Club,' he said. 'Why did Faber let you?'

'I don't think he even noticed my departure.'

'So what made you do such a damn-fool thing?' At her frown he elaborated, 'Take a midnight swim in a deserted pool on a roughish night while the ship ploughed through the North Atlantic Ocean?'

She could have answered him, 'Calvin sitting there just tolerating my company. You dancing so intimately with your fiancée. You, always mocking me, just the sight of you tormenting me, and in a day and a half's time, you deserting me ... for ever.'

'I went for a walk,' she said at last. 'It was slippery. The ship rolled and I slid right down into the water.'

He might have laughed, but his face was serious. 'You were near to drowning.' She nodded. 'I came out because I thought I heard someone call my name.'

'You heard, over the noise of the music and the people?'

'I heard. Through my brain, not my ears. Sixth sense?' His hand came out and rested casually on her stomach. His face registered no feeling, but by the way he looked at her she guessed that he was testing her reaction to his touch.

She closed her eyes as her brain struggled for supremacy over her physical sensations. Telepathy? she considered, revelling in the exquisite excitement of his touch. Are we as sensitive as that to each other? If we are, then why should that woman have him? Why couldn't it be me? She pushed away the hand that was causing such havoc with her bodily responses, grabbed the cover again, cocooning herself in it, and of necessity rolling in his direction. What has she got that I haven't? she wondered miserably. Slowly and with painful clarity, her brain spelled out exactly what the blonde model, Marguerite, did possess. And you, it told her, have a reasonably good brain and a piano-playing technique polished enough to make a captive instant-response audience clamour for more ...

Which, she summed up silently with a sigh, was why Marguerite was his fiancée and she, Shona Carroll, was not.

'Please, Marsh,' she said into the pillow, 'will you lend me something to wear so that I can go back to my cabin?'

The mattress eased as he stood. 'A shirt and a towelling robe?' A few moments later, fingers began peeling the bedcovers away, but she clung on to them, looking up at him defiantly.

'Just give them to me, will you? I'll put them on.'

The cover was tugged down and she hurriedly crossed her arms over herself. Marsh said, with an air of tried patience, 'I've seen almost all there is to see about you, and the rest is hardly difficult for a man like me to imagine— especially with the scrap of material you wear to maintain your womanly dignity. So quit the innocent maiden performance. The audience is unimpressed. Sit up.'

The order was issued curtly, divesting it of all feeling. Shona found herself obeying, but still trying to hide her upper half.

'Loosen your arms,' he said on a long-suffering sigh. 'And stop looking at me like a domestic pet that doesn't know whether its master is going to stroke it or strike it.' His eyes raked her body. 'Speaking as a man, my primitive instincts are urging me to do both.'

With cool amusement he watched the colour rise until Shona's flesh burned—not, she realised with dismay, with embarrassment, but a pulsating desire.

'But with an almighty effort,' his hand reached out to rest on her midriff, and she did not draw back, 'I'll check them until——' He broke off abruptly and commanded her to slip her arms into the shirt's sleeves.

As she fumbled with the buttons, she looked around.

'Have you got the robe?' His head shook negatively. 'I don't believe you!' she burst out. 'How can I walk all that way back like this?'

'I've no intention of letting you.'

'What do you mean?' Her question was a whisper.

'You've just come through something of an ordeal, so what's left of the night you're spending right here in that bed, where I can keep an eye on you.'

She saw that the other bed had been turned down by the steward. The one she occupied had been left untouched. 'I don't need your eyes on me. I'm perfectly all right.'

'Try walking.'

She swung her legs to the floor, conscious of his eyes on her long limbs. As her feet found the carpet, she felt their weakness. The ship rolled and she grabbed the bed. 'That wasn't me, that was——'

He was beside her at once. 'Never give up, do you?' His arms had scooped her up, the bedclothes were pulled back and she was dumped in the bed, the covers being spread across her. 'Go to sleep, my sour puss. Maybe by morning I'll be able to call you "my sweet puss".'

'Marsh, what will your fiancée say? I can't spend the night here with you!'

'She'll understand when I explain. What about your fiancé?' The question was drawled. 'Will he come banging on my door demanding retribution for his wife-to-be's lost virtue?'

'He's not my fiancé,' she said, sinking back wearily.

'Another lovers' quarrel? Is that how you'll spend all your married life?' He was stripping for bed, pulling off his shirt, unfastening his belt.

'Please, Marsh,' she said, aghast, and turning her head away, 'if you sleep in the nude, I——'

There was a long silence. 'Okay, you can look. Out of respect for your extraordinary show of maidenly modesty, I'll keep my underpants on.'

Slowly her head turned, then her heart turned over at the masculinity of him, the broad shoulders, the melting, magnetic good looks. She swallowed. 'Are you going to wash?'

'I showered after drying you, while you were asleep.' He got into bed, then saw that he hadn't turned out her bed-light. He swung out and came over to her, found the switch, glanced down and asked, 'Okay?'

Her heart was pounding so that she could hardly hear. Instead of nodding her head shook 'no'. His eyebrows lifted in query. 'A goodnight kiss? Okay by me, sweet-heart.' His mouth approached hers with a slowness that almost drove her mad.

'Marsh,' she choked, and reached up to pull him the rest of the way. He took over and the kiss was thorough but light.

'Oh, no,' he said firmly, as she held on to him. 'Oh no, sweetheart. You belong to Faber.' He loosened her arms and she dropped back to the pillows.

'And you,' she said dully, 'belong to Marguerite.'

It was a statement he did not dispute. He got into his own bed. There was a long silence, broken by the sound of the ship's engines, the air-conditioning, a sound or two from the corridor.

'Marsh? Are you asleep?'

'No.'

'It's true what I said about Calvin and me. There's no engagement.' A long pause. 'I couldn't marry him, not now.' She waited. 'We did quarrel, after my performance with Danny. Calvin said it was terrible, I was awful, the concerto—it was rubbish. I shouted at him, he shouted back. Then I accused him of jealousy, and——' How could she go on, telling this disinterested man all her secrets?

'Go on.'

The darkness was neutral, inviting confidences. 'And he cried, Marsh. Then I knew, I understood—everything, about him, about my feelings towards him.' Another silence. 'I'm sorry for him, Marsh. He's brilliant, he'll go a long way. But,' she propped herself on her elbow, 'you can't marry a man you pity, can you, Marsh? Pity's not love.'

'No, it's not love.' He sounded as if he were tired—of her prattling? Of listening to the outpourings of her private problems?

Well, she wouldn't trouble him any longer. In fact, she'd pretend to go to sleep, then she'd slip out of bed, drape the bedcover around her and race along to the lift and return to her own cabin.

So she went silent, listening for the tempo of his breathing to change to the relaxed regularity of sleep. When she was convinced in every way that he slept, she eased from the bed, lifted the cover by feeling in the darkness, folded it roughly and swung it round her. As she crept across the cabin the ship tilted and she paused until it steadied, reaching out at last for the door lock.

She was so absorbed in turning the lock quietly, she had not heard over the sound of the air-conditioning the movements behind her. 'What the hell do you think you're doing?' The voice was so close she juddered with surprise.

She turned, putting her back to the door. 'You can't make me stay, you can't! I might not have the freedom of a fare-paying passenger, but you haven't bought me with that contract I signed.' He towered over her and her hands felt the door for support. The bedcover slipped and then fell away. 'You can't make me stay, Marsh ...' There was defiance in her voice which she immediately regretted, cursing herself for not having remembered that a defiant attitude often acted as a challenge.

Its effect was immediate. Marsh's hands shot out and fastened on her hips. Knowing where they were must have been pure instinct, since there was darkness all around them. He jerked her to him, running his hands over the contours of her body, roughly at first, lightening to a stroking caress which made her want to cry out in exquisite longing.

But she compressed her lips and kept in the cry, gasping as his hands crept beneath the loose shirt and moved inexorably upwards until they cupped her breasts. When he pressed himself against her, thus pressing his own hands even closer on to her swelling shape, the cry leapt out only to be captured again by the ruthless pressure of his lips.

At the moment she knew her legs would soon cease to support her, he withdrew his plundering mouth and whispered, 'Do you still want to go?'

For a moment she could not trust herself to speak. 'How can I stay?' she said at last. 'You've got a fiancée. Even if in your world it's done to take another woman while you're engaged to another, in my world it isn't.'

'Is that what you think would happen if you stayed?' he asked, his voice strange. 'Try me, try my self control.' With which words, he lifted her into his arms and carried her to the bed.

Reaction set in—to the fall in the pool, the near-drowning, his kisses and caresses, her presence in his cabin in the night—and she started to shake. 'Oh, Marsh,' she said through her chattering teeth, 'I c-can't s-stop. W-what can I d-do?'

He eased her over and got in beside her, wrapping his arms around her and pulling her into his warmth. 'Does that help, my sweet?'

After a while, the trembling was stilled and her body became tranquil. The warmth blanketed her mind and muffled her thoughts and she surrendered to sleep.

Night was over, she could tell by the sweet relaxation of her limbs. Even though the room was still in darkness, she knew she had finished sleeping.

She stirred and found herself in a man's arms. Whose——? 'Marsh.' She had said his name instead of thinking it. Then the night's events came rushing back. Her head turned quickly to find the face of the man sharing her pillow.

He stirred at once and she felt he was smiling. Her fingers came up to test the curve of his mouth. When his hand removed hers and his mouth sought out and found her lips, she was lost. Thoughts of Marguerite invaded the kiss, stiffening her limbs and deadening her responses.

The touch of him inflamed her, but she struggled to free herself.

'I've lost you,' he said, pressing his hand against the back of her head. 'Come back to me.'

'No, no, I can't. You know what it would lead to and I'm not——'

'In your world it's not done,' he mocked.

'Relieve your masculine frustrations with your fiancée's co-operation,' she flung back, trying to prise his hand from her hip.

'My darling, that's exactly what I'm trying to do. Isn't it?'

Shona was still, yet her heart kept beating—so hard it almost shook her. So fast did the blood course through her veins, she was sure he could feel it, too. 'I don't know what you mean.' Her words were breathy, as if her lips were refusing to work.

'I mean that it's you I'm going to marry, not Marguerite, not any other woman.' Now her speech had deserted her. She could only wait for him to continue. 'Marguerite came on board to model for the company's new advertising brochure. We've known each other, as friends, for some time. I asked her to act as my fiancée.'

Shona said incredulously, 'To do for you what you tried to do for me?'

'Clever of you to work it out, my lovely.'

'Why, you——' Her hand came up, but his reaction was so fast she had no chance to bring it down on target. With her wrist in his grip, she said, 'You tried to make me jealous. You——'

'Tried? Succeeded. Be honest with me.'

'But you knew about Calvin and me. You kept calling him my fiancé——'

'After I saw you sitting together on the bed, with *his* head on *your* shoulder, I knew that whatever was between you—very little as far as I could judge—couldn't last.'

'So you thought you had a clear field where I was concerned.'

'I didn't think, I knew. And when a man loves a woman as I, my love, love you, he lets nothing, but nothing, stand in his way.'

'Marsh Faraday, what you don't deserve . . .'

He jerked her towards him and when their bodies touched there was inside Shona an explosion of desire which, as it mixed with the overwhelming love she felt for him, proved a powerful and intoxicating concoction indeed.

'I know what you deserve,' he said, and his hand reached out to close her lips which were opened on a gasp of protest. 'Marriage to me, and that's what you're going to get.'

'Are you proposing?' she asked, her body trembling now for a different reason.

'Not proposing—informing, demanding, stating. And you're agreeing. Right?'

Her brown eyes melted as they gazed into his. 'You're dictatorial and overbearing and you're a tyrant, Marsh Faraday, but——' she curled into him, 'I love you so much and I've loved you from the moment——' her head came up, 'the moment we were pressed against each other the day we left Southampton——'

He laughed, his face lighting up at the memory.

'That the only thing I can say is,' she told him, 'yes, yes, please.'

With joy she accepted his betrothal kiss and when, with reluctance, he ended it, he said,

'I told you I had self-control and so far I've proved it. I'm exercising it now, my love. But if we don't get out of this bed this minute, I can't vouch for its holding much longer. Come with me and I'll show you something.'

He pushed the covers aside and pulled on pants and a shirt. He threw her a silk robe which he took from his bedside chair. Pulling open a drawer, he took out a piece of paper.

'Come and read this, my sweet musician. It's a message the radio operator took for me over the ship's radio last night.'

His arm round her waist pulled her close and he told her,

'When I heard you play and realised the extent of your musical ability, I contacted, via the ship's radio—when we were in port at Gibraltar—a friend of mine. He's a well-known impresario. He says,' Marsh read the message, 'Bring your beautiful discovery to my office on your return. Am looking for new, young talent for the London concert circuit. Will give her an audition. She had better be as good as you say! And beautiful. Regards, Joss Wadsworth.' He put the typewritten message down. 'How's that for a good morning greeting?'

'Oh, Marsh!' Shona was too choked to say more and let her body do it for her. Her arms reached up and imprisoned his neck. He went willingly down as she tugged. For a few seconds he tolerated the light kisses she was giving him. Then he took over and it was a long time before her lips were free to whisper the words, 'How can I thank you?'

'I'll tell you how, my darling, when the right time comes. Now I'll show you something else.' He led her to the windows and pulled aside the curtains.

The yellow sphere crept from below a misty, mysterious horizon. First the sky caught the golden rays, then the sea rippled with their reflection. Shona gazed up at Marsh in wonderment as he said, holding her as if he would never let her go,

'There it comes—the sun rising on the first morning of the rest of our lives together.'

Harlequin understands how you feel about Love...

Harlequin novels are stories of people in love—people like you—and all are beautiful romances set in exotic faraway places.

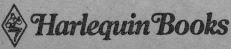

◆ *Harlequin Books*

Available at your favorite bookstore.

What the press says about Harlequin romance fiction...

"...light entertainment well-larded with
enlightenment.... Romance is a grand
concept, an important part of life."
    — *Eagle*, Lawrence (Mass.)

"The most popular reading matter of
American women today."
    — *Detroit News*

"Women have come to trust these
stories about contemporary people,
set in exciting foreign places."
    —*Best Sellers*, New York

"Harlequin novels have a vast and
loyal readership."
    — *Toronto Star*

FREE!
Romance Treasury

**A beautifully bound,
value-packed,
three-in-one
volume of romance!**

FREE!

A hardcover Romance Treasury volume
containing 3 treasured works of romance
by 3 outstanding Harlequin authors...

...as your introduction to Harlequin's
Romance Treasury subscription plan!

Romance Treasury

**...almost 600 pages of exciting romance reading
every month at the low cost of $5.97 a volume!**

A wonderful way to collect many of Harlequin's most beautiful love
stories, all originally published in the late '60s and early '70s.
Each value-packed volume, bound in a distinctive gold-embossed
leatherette case and wrapped in a colorfully illustrated dust jacket,
contains...
- 3 full-length novels by 3 world-famous authors of romance fiction
- a unique illustration for every novel
- the elegant touch of a delicate bound-in ribbon bookmark...
  and much, much more!

Romance Treasury

...for a library of romance you'll treasure forever!

Complete and mail today the FREE gift certificate and subscription
reservation on the following page.

Romance Treasury

An exciting opportunity to collect treasured works of romance! Almost 600 pages of exciting romance reading in each beautifully bound hardcover volume!

You may cancel your subscription whenever you wish! You don't have to buy any minimum number of volumes. Whenever you decide to stop your subscription just drop us a line and we'll cancel all further shipments.

FREE GIFT!
Certificate and Subscription Reservation

Mail this coupon today to
Harlequin Reader Service

In U.S.A.
MPO Box 707
Niagara Falls, NY 14302

In Canada
649 Ontario St.
Stratford, Ontario N5A 6W2

Please send me my FREE Romance Treasury volume. Also, reserve a subscription to the new Romance Treasury published every month. Each month I will receive a Romance Treasury volume at the low price of $5.97 plus .49¢ for postage and handling (total—$6.46). There are no shipping and handling or any other hidden charges. I am free to cancel at any time, but if I do, my FREE Romance Treasury volume is mine to keep, without any obligation.

NAME _____
(Please Print)

ADDRESS _____

CITY _____

STATE/PROV. _____

ZIP/POSTAL CODE _____

Offer expires November 30, 1981.   B2404
Offer not valid to present subscribers.